NOCTURNE, SON OF THE NIGHT

AJ Cooper

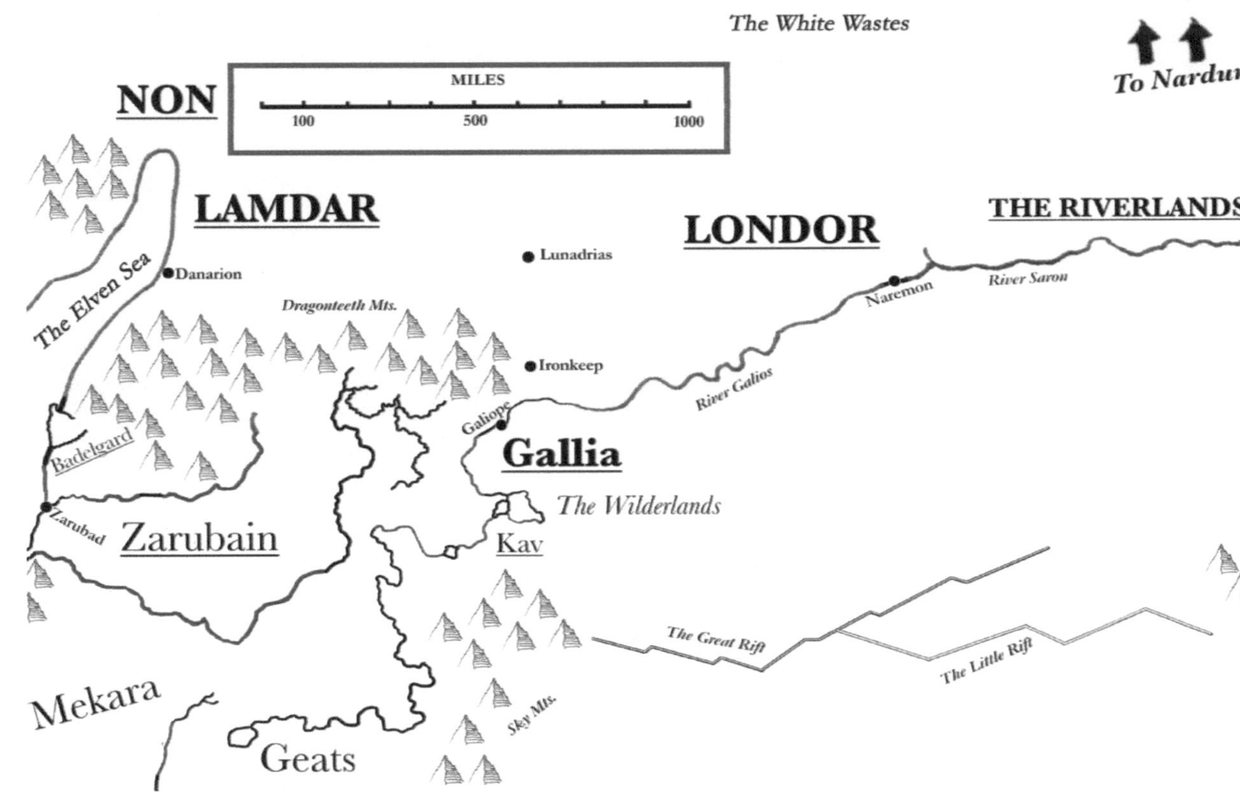

NON
LAMDAR
LONDOR
THE RIVERLANDS
The White Wastes
To Nardur
MILES
100
500
1000
The Elven Sea
Danarion
Lunadrias
Dragonteeth Mts.
Naremon
River Saron
Ironkeep
River Galios
Badelgard
Galiope
Gallia
The Wilderlands
Zarubad
Zarubain
Kav
Mekara
Geats
Sky Mts.
The Great Rift
The Little Rift

PRAISE FOR NOCTURNE, SON OF THE NIGHT

"[The] main character, Nocturne, is engaging and well-drawn... Cooper has created an intriguing and vivid fantasy world with a lot of plausible detail about its geography, weather, local economy, diverse species and relationships... [This book] is one of those Candide-type stories about the wanderer in search of himself and is quite compelling."
—Inanna Arthen, author of **Mortal Touch**

CHAPTER ONE: NO JOY IN BLOOD

Monsters—that's what outsiders call us. Human or otherwise, they never come to our lands; they only murmur in dim-lit taverns, telling horror stories over glasses of ale. They turn my race, the druen, into bloodsucking murderers, and their skills at fabrication know no limit. But despite this, I like to think my heart, though it does not beat, is far from dead.

I grew up in a fishing village on the coast. Drastheon is small, but I've always been proud of my town. We do not practice the dark rites of the capital, where the soldiers sacrifice every firstborn child as a bloodmeal to the rich.

Of course, if we did practice that rite, my family would benefit. As a member of the House Rabaam, I resided in the largest home in Drastheon. Our home, simply called "The Manor," was sprawling and huge, composed of stone, with a red tile roof. It lay toward the outskirts of town. The out-of-town royals and bards often remarked favorably about Manor's innards. We had only the finest furnishings: glass cups, painted porcelain dishes, varnished teak furniture, and ornamental eggs. Despite this, we tried to withhold our pretensions; some of the less fortunate in Drastheon despised us for our luck. But it really wasn't luck, you see.

My grandfather was responsible for it all. My parents named me after him: Dralynthi. Nocturne. He was a well-known entrepreneur. His business consisted of the purchase and sale of slaves—mostly elven slaves, but sometimes humans picked from the far reaches. They would cook, or clean, or sleep with their masters, but their lives always ended as a blood meals, when they grew old or ineffectual. This had been the fate of all our family slaves—Men and elves, girls and boys.

I was twenty years old, one unseasonably cold day in what should have been late spring. A deep layer of snow covered the roofs of the houses and huts.

A cluster of ramshackle buildings surrounded the village square. In the center was a stand where I could always find the fishmonger. He sold haddock, fresh blue haddock, every day. He sold his produce every day, without fail, except for feast-days. He'd been in the trade since before I was born.

Right beside him, just a few yards away, I noticed something different: a wooden cage. It was composed of varnished pinewood bars. Yet the thing inside was the most interesting part. A human stood there. She was about my age. She looked young, and her skin was smooth and un-blistered by work. Her hair, a dark brown, hung to her hips in a long ponytail. Her thin, dark brows complemented her deep blue eyes perfectly. And yet her demeanor struck me, most of all.

Most slaves shook and cried and begged for freedom, when they came to druen lands. They never earned our sympathy.

Yet this girl was not afraid. She had a look that seemed to say, "Try me."

As my gaze upon her lingered, my reaction surprised me. A deep desire overcame me. She was the most beautiful creature I'd ever seen. I knew very little of her, truly, but I imagined everything else: strong and un-submissive, but with a good heart behind the iron shell.

Humans were off limits as wives. Having any meaningful relationship with her would brand me as a traitor to my pure elvish race. This aversion to human relations was common among all the Elf Tribes—but with the druen, doing so carried the penalty of death. Yet looking at this girl—this slave—did more things to me than any person I had ever met in Drastheon or elsewhere.

"Nocturne!" shouted a voice I knew very well. The voice

of my neighbor, Dreddani. The salutation was accompanied, as I expected, by a pungent wave of body odor.

I suppressed a groan. "Dreddani," I said.

"Cold day, eh?"

"Yes."

"Strange weather for this late in the year, eh?"

"Yes."

"Snow's sure pilin' up, eh?"

I said nothing. Neither did he, for a while. I thanked every god and spirit whenever Dreddani's mouth was shut. Such rare occasions were a divine gift. I say this only as a matter of speech; I do not believe in the gods, or that anything should be called a god.

Dreddani spoke again; proof for my disbelief. "Pretty good lookin' slave they got there. She'd make a good maid. O' course, she might very well do more than cleanin', eh? Eh?"

I sighed.

"I got three crowns saved up. I might buy her, maybe, if no one wants her."

"You're too poor to outbid me," I said.

"You want her?" Dreddani put one of his meaty hands on my shoulder.

I flinched. "Not necessarily."

"Well, then I might buy her. I might bed her and then drink 'er dry."

I shook his hand off my shoulder and snarled. "That is an incredible waste, Dreddani! A complete waste of a healthy slave. Three crowns for one night of fun, and a good dinner—doesn't that sound impulsive? And incredibly idiotic?"

"Well, I don't know."

I struck him hard with my hand and he yelped. I headed back home. And completely forgot about dinner.

My mother, Drassané, threw a fit when she saw my empty hands. "Nocturne Gangimmi Emorthi Drethuli Rabaam!"

I had long learned to block out her shrill voice. She was old and old-fashioned, in her late 160s. She wore a necklace of pearls and paid excessive attention to her graying hair.

My father was similarly old and old-fashioned, in his early 200s, and had a very antiquated view on life: Marry only a druen from your home village; lie with one woman, your wife; do not drink the blood of your fellow druen. Control your bloodlust and only drink when you must, and when it is appropriate and civil.

"You must march right back and get us our dinner," Mother said, and sighed. "Oh, Nocturne, you're so scatterbrained."

I nodded. "Yes, mother." I turned and opened the door a crack.

"I love you, Nocturne."

"I love you too, Mother."

The fishmonger's produce was crusted over by ice. Only eight fish remained. The slave girl stood a few yards away, her hands grasping the bars.

I approached the fishmonger briskly. "I'll have some haddock."

Scars covered every inch of the fisherman's face. He always had the appearance of biting into a sour grape. "Four for two silver," he said. "By the way, this girl's three crowns. Nice deal, if I do say so myself."

"You're selling her?" I asked.

"Yeh. Came by this morning," said the fishmonger. "Three crowns, that's it."

I trudged up to the girl. I was a little nervous. "What's your name?" I said.

Her eyes narrowed. She frowned. "My name is 'Shut-Your-Fangs.'"

I smiled faintly. She had boundless energy, something good for a wife. But this marriage would have to be secret.

"What's your name, really?" I asked.

"Go away," she said.

I walked over and tossed two silver coins onto the fishmonger's table. Then I walked back to the cage and said, "I'm Nocturne." I reached through the cage bars and forced her to look at me. I said, "You are pretty."

"Don't make me hit you," she said, eyeing my groin.

I ran my fingers along her cheek. "You are so tense," I said.

She jerked away. "I'll scream, if you touch me again."

"What good would that do?"

The fishmonger called out, "Nocturne! You gonna take your haddock, or you gonna sit there 'n flirt? Come on!"

He successfully redirected my attention. I grabbed a handful of the frozen haddock. Hopefully, Mother would make a good dinner tonight.

Mother served the pan-fried haddock on silver plates. It was delicious. But my thoughts drifted constantly, back to the slave and how cheaply I could free her. And how no one had ever drawn me in so strongly. What did I have to lose? I had everything to gain.

She was rude, but perhaps if she got to know me, she would like me more. By the time I had placed the last bit of haddock in my mouth, and drank the last drop of mead from my cup, I had made my decision.

I would march straight back to the village square and purchase her for the three crowns she was going for.

Yet when I returned, she was gone. The fishmonger was packing up his wooden table, apparently ready to go home.

"What happened to the girl?" I asked. I clutched the three gold coins in my fingers, feeling like a fool.

"Oh, her?" he asked. "Eh, Dreddani bought 'er. You're too late."

"Dreddani!" The fat bastard would probably do what he said he would—lie with her and drink her dry. She deserved more than that fat pig, even if she was human. She deserved an upstanding druen from a good family, someone who thought more of her than as a bloodmeal. She deserved me.

I dashed down the road, as fast as I could. Snowflakes drifted from the sky with blinding number, and a freezing wind blasted out of the sea. I ran down the road, knowing that I had very little time. It took only a minute or so to fully drink a human's blood. I sprinted as hard as I could, but my legs just wouldn't carry me any faster.

I passed by the Manor, where my mother and father were doubtlessly reclining, unaware of the slave-girl's plight. Dreddani's house was a short run from there. I continued my sprint, knowing I'd soon collapse in exhaustion; I wasn't used to running. Finally, I arrived.

Someone screamed from inside Dreddani's shack. I dashed at the door, blood boiling in my veins. My fangs contracted of their own accord. I dashed to his doorstep and gave it a powerful kick, but it wouldn't budge. I kicked it again and again. With each kick the door splintered; the hinges shuddered and weakened.

Dreddani's voice called out from within. "Who the hell is it?"

"Help me!" screamed the slave-girl.

I kicked harder than ever and the door gave way, splitting open with a loud crack. Dreddani had his fangs sunk into the girl's neck, drinking her down fast. My mind burned, my hands shook, with anger.

I charged at him, and ripped him away. Two puncture-holes pocked the slave-girl's neck.

I sank my fangs into his neck. Felt his blood rush up through my gums. The high was indescribable. The arousing blood took my mind soaring to unthinkable heights. I drank deeply, as Dreddani struggled against me. For a second, I thought I could understand the passion of the Morthen, who dedicated their life to pursuing the druen's greatest pleasure.

I continued until Dreddani weakened. He was fat and out of shape, and soon his legs gave out. And yet, once I had drunk the last drop of blood, I questioned the immense pleasure. The unfulfilling sensation seemed so pointless. Regret overcame me and I realized there is no joy in blood.

The girl was ashen-faced. She had fallen onto the floor, her body gone limp. I would rescue her. I would take care of her. I grabbed her and lifted her into my arms, letting her head recline on my shoulder.

I staggered outside into the blinding snow. It seemed like the darkest depths of winter had come once again, with its endless nights and penetrating cold. Down the road, I saw a village boy running towards town screaming about my betrayal. Soon, the whole village be roused. I was a traitor; I had murdered a druen for the sake of a slave.

I dashed through the doors of the Manor with the slave in my arms. I frantically told my mother what happened, as I held the slave's unconscious body.

The tears started pouring. "Oh, Nocturne, you fool! You damnable fool! They'll kill you, you know. You damned foolish boy." She sobbed. "Oh, they'll kill you now. Why in the world would you do this? Run, Nocturne. And don't forget me."

"I could never forget you, Mother."

I set her down briefly and ran for the closet. I grabbed a large bearskin coat and wrapped the slave-girl within it. Humans, unlike druen, can die from cold weather. I went to the kitchen, and grabbed a satchel full of dried fish.

Then, I left.

The town sounded the alarm. They grabbed daggers and knives and fishing-spears; whatever they could kill me with. They ran out of their homes to look for me, but I slipped into the taiga. I ran into the forest eaves with Katrina in my arms.

I had betrayed my race for a human girl. As I dashed into the icy pine forest, I knew what I had done. I had sacrificed my life on a whim. I had ruined any chance of living in Drastheon.

I had made the right decision.

CHAPTER TWO: A TRAITOR TO MY PEOPLE

I ventured either north or south; for the setting sun was to my side. I entered the Great Taiga that filled all of Nardur except the civilized places.

I went fifteen minutes without realizing that Katrina was unprotected, that the bearskin on my back was not around her. She was shivering, and her pale skin was white and cold to the touch. I wrapped the bearskin tight around her shoulders and then carefully hoisted her back in my arms.

The icy chill knifed into my skin like needles, and the snow accumulated fast. Already four inches covered the ground; the arctic wind blasting out of the sea seared my skin like fire, and the sky was darkening. All around me lay towering dark green pines and the rock-strewn ground. This was not grizzly country, but there were other things to be concerned about. Gray wolves were known to roam here, and the Morthen sometimes strayed into the Great Taiga in their endless quest for blood.

I searched for shelter for perhaps an hour, trudging through the blinding snow. I knew that traveling any further would be deadly in this blizzard. Eventually I came to a small cave. It offered good protection from the wind, which, more than the air, made things feel so cold.

I rushed deep into the cave mouth and set poor, shivering Katrina down. She was still unconscious.

Thinking she needed more layers, I removed my coat and wrapped it around Katrina's shoulders. I was left in nothing more than a light tunic. I huddled near her, adding to her warmth with my body. Then I waited for hours.

Eventually she awoke, and I had not yet fallen asleep. She stirred slightly. "So thirsty," she said, her voice only a faint whisper. She slumped onto my shoulder again. I needed to get her some water and fast.

"Hold on a moment," I said. I had a leather flask around my neck, which I had always kept for when I got thirsty, but it was empty. Finding water wouldn't be hard, if I broke through the ice of Nardur's many streams. I had a strong arm, and the ice had gotten thinner since midwinter.

It took me less than five minutes before I found a stream, the water frozen as it ran down the hill. As I wandered through the silent forest, left only to my thoughts as the snow fell down, I wondered if I truly had made the right decision.

I punched deep into the water until the ice was shattered, until I felt the frigid water touch my hand. Dipping my hand into numbing water, I filled the flask until the water stopped its bubbling. Then I pulled it out, exposing my wet hand to the freezing wind, and struggled to plug the stopper.

Katrina drank slowly. The water was ice cold, but she needed every drop. Dreddani had drained a lot of blood from her. I made sure she drank every last dribble. Then I scooted beside her and put my arm around her neck.

Her eyes opened and she shrieked. She threw my arm off of her. "Where are we? Who are you?"

"We are in a cave, Katrina," I said, trying my best to sound firm. "We are safe from the druen."

"The monsters... they took me to their village... the monster, he almost killed me... you... you're a monster," she said. "Get off me!"

"I'm not one of them!" I said, barely containing a growl. "Stop thinking! You need to relax!"

"I don't talk to vampires!" she said. "You're all evil bloodsuckers! Get away from me and don't kill me."

"I don't want to kill you!" I answered frantically. "If I wanted to, I would have finished the job already."

"Hmmph!" She scooted a few feet away from me, wrapping the bearskin tight around her body. Within moments she had fallen asleep.

I scooted a few feet away and growled to myself. As my blood boiled, I pondered the old adage: that no good deed goes unpunished. And that Katrina, once wonderful to my eyes, was quite mean-spirited.

I awoke just after dawn. I thought about just leaving her here, since she was so unappreciative, but I found myself tapping her on the shoulder. Katrina grumbled something indistinct in sleep-talk, then awoke.

She regained her consciousness slowly. "What is it?" she said at last.

"You need to eat," I said. I opened the satchel and threw a salted haddock into her lap.

"I don't like fish," she said.

"Well if you'd rather starve, that's perfectly fine by me!" I hissed. "Or wait. I'm sorry! You wanted the cooked crab legs that grow on the trees out in the taiga, and the sweet mead that flows here in rivers."

"I don't like mead," she said. "I prefer wine. And crabs count as fish."

I grabbed the haddock and firmly held it up to her lips. I held it there until she realized she had no choice. Taking it in her frail fingers she began chewing. Inside the satchel, there were about ten left; enough to last a few days.

I watched her until she finished. "You're welcome," I growled.

"I didn't thank you," she said hoarsely. She was still very weak from the blood loss, struggling to move her hands. She shook ever so slightly as she took bites out of the haddock, but she finished it just the same.

"Now you have two options," I said, trying my best to contain my anger. "I can carry you away from here in my arms. Or you can die in the icy, blistering cold."

She said nothing and I took her silence as affirmation. I hoisted her into my arms, covered in the bearskin, and left the cave.

Though I did not know the direction, I began following a frozen stream that meandered through the taiga. I recall long ago, in my youth, a hunter telling me that almost every village in Nardur, perhaps nine out of ten, was located very near a stream or body of water. So I thereby concluded that if I followed this little trickle to its source, I'd find a town where we could rest, or at least get better supplies.

Again I tried to be friendly to her. "Where do you come from?"

"Not talking," she grunted.

"I saved your life!" I said.

"Your friend almost killed me."

"Dreddani isn't my friend. Nothing close," I answered. "And secondly, he didn't succeed. And thirdly, I killed him, by the gods; I destroyed my life to save you. Maybe I should have let him drink you dry."

Katrina glared with unexplainable hatred.

I thought about leaving her in the wilderness, but for some reason I didn't. I still clung to some semblance of the old ways, of my father's teachings. A real man treats women well and never harms them.

As snowflakes fell and dusk overcame the forest, I set Katrina against a tree and started building a shelter out of sticks and pine boughs. I was no woodsman, but I managed to build it. I angled the logs and sticks against each other to build a triangular structure. Then, when the bare bones of the shelter were completed, I tore the bristly boughs off the pines and layered them across the logs to act as a roof.

As I built the shelter, I thought quietly, remembering the Manor and its luxuriant amenities, its warm rugs and its spacious hearths. And that now, I, an outcast, was building a temporary shelter out of pine boughs for a woman who would never appreciate anything I did.

I remembered my mother and my father and the people of the village. I kept building.

Inside, we were safe from the snow, but we were unprotected from each other.

"Is this how you treat everyone who saves your life?" I asked her. "Everyone who builds a shelter for you in the middle of the forest?"

"You only saved me because you thought you could have me," Katrina said. "And you can't."

"You grow less desirable to me every day," I answered.

"Well I don't want to talk," Katrina said. "It's getting late. Shouldn't you be out prowling for dinner?"

"I already have my dinner right here, in front of me," I threatened. I let my fangs protract.

For a second she looked scared, but her expression hardened into a sneer. "You couldn't harm a flea," she said.

"You are much less valuable to me than a flea," I answered. "I think we should part ways. I'm leaving you here in the morning and I don't care what you have to say about it."

She looked into my eyes, an insult hovering on the tip of her tongue. But her teeth clamped down. Her gaze softened and she eyed the ground. "I was being harsh," she said, "I'll go with you."

I watched her as she lay down on the bearskin, scooted around to get comfortable, and shut her eyes. She curled in her makeshift bed sheets.

I heard tears and sniffling. Eventually she fell silent, drifting off to sleep.

We traveled the next day in complete silence. As the stream meandered, the forest changed very little. The Great Taiga was a sprawling forest composed of billowing pines and layered in an impenetrable blanket of snow, except midsummer. Grizzlies used to live here, but hunters had driven them out long ago. Now the grizzly bears lived a little north of Drastheon.

I did not like the outdoors, I preferred settlement. I liked the city. I had never understood people who enjoyed being in the middle of nowhere, in a forest full of dangerous beasts where there was nothing to do and nothing to see except trees and snow.

Perhaps I could not appreciate for the gods' handiwork— a phrase I only use as a matter of speech, because I do not believe that invisible gods in the sky exist, nor do I believe that anything in heaven or earth is worthy of the title "god."

As I carried ungrateful Katrina in my arms, we said nothing. Our only interactions were done in silence. Sometimes, seeing the dirty looks she gave me, I thought of drinking her dry, or at the very least leaving her to her fate. But I kept carrying her through the woods because behind all those looks of condescension was a genuine desperation.

A few hours after noon, I caught sight of dark snow-clouds. Soon snowflakes began drifting down in such great number that I could scarcely see two feet in front of me. So I looked for a place to stay the night that was sheltered from the snow. I didn't want to build a tent again; I didn't have the patience for it today.

I found a rocky cave carved out of a hill, just a few yards away from the frozen stream we were following.

I hurried into the cave, carrying Katrina in my arms as a violent, icy wind picked up and the blizzard totally blinded me. I laid her down against the uneven stone and took out the burlap sack of fish.

Slumping down, I grabbed a salted haddock from the satchel and threw it at her. The fish bounced off her face and I laughed. I grabbed one for myself and took a giant bite. I liked haddock, but long-preserved, salty haddock was not as good as my mother's pan-fried recipes.

As I ate, I remembered there were two of us. Our eyes met.

"Don't look at me like that," Katrina said.

"Like what?"

"Like you're going to suck my blood. Like you're going to finish the job your fat friend started! Like you're going to drink me dry."

"I wasn't planning on it. But if you keep up the attitude, maybe I'll consider it."

She raised her hand to strike me. I grabbed it and she softened, loosening up like gelatin. Her eyes softened. Her lips trembled and her eyes moistened.

I looked down and let her be.

"I'm sorry," she whispered, "so sorry, Nocturne."

I brushed her back. "It's okay, Katrina," I said.

"I'm just so frightened."

"You don't have to be scared of me."

"I know," she said, her voice shaking. "The slavers…they took me away from my home to this… this god-awful place. It's just so hard for me to trust one of you."

"Hush," I said. "Go to sleep. You need the rest."

She fell asleep against my shoulder.

I woke up and she was clutching me like a rock in a depthless sea, one hand on my shoulder, one hand on my arm. I was slick with sweat, although I didn't know if it was hers or mine.

I shook her awake. "We have to keep moving and find a settlement."

No condescension could be seen in her eyes, only a tender, emotionless pall.

"All right," she said. "Let's go."

"I didn't give you a chance," Katrina said as we walked.

"I accept your apology," I answered. "I didn't think about how different things are for you up here, how hard it must be for you to trust a druen. There are many rumors about us. That we are ravenous bloodsuckers…"

"You *are* ravenous bloodsuckers," Katrina said flatly.

"Most of us, I guess."

"You too."

I smiled. As I walked, legs sore from travel, I asked her questions about her past, wanting to know more about her.

"How did you end up in Drastheon?" I asked her.

"It started when I was working on my father's vineyard," she said. Her breath, blowing against me, smelled of salt from the dried fish. "I hated working there and so did my friend Bree," she continued, her voice having strengthened since yesterday. "One day we decided to run off. We ran maybe ten miles up the Galios River… then the boat of elves came. They were slave-traders. They caught us. And then they sold us to a different pair of slavers for a couple of silver coins. Then Bree and I got separated. She got sold to Nart— Narth— Narthar—"

"Narthariom," I said, "That's quite far away."

"And I got sold—"

"Across the sea to Port Andom, then to Druenel-Hai, and finally Drastheon. Along the usual slave route."

"Yes," she breathed. "That journey was horrible. Bree's journey was short. But they took me all the way north into the arctic. I hate it… the wind, the cold!"

"Tell me about your home village, Galiope."

"Well," she said. "It's not really a village, it's more a city. Some folks call it the Jewel of the North. Of course, it's probably not as grand or beautiful as any of the other great cities faraway. But I lived in the country, actually, outside the walls. We Galiopeans don't have a king or a queen, we've got a council and a mayor. It's not as big as other cities—I think it was thirty thousand people at the last census, if I remember right."

"A city does not have to be big to be great," I said. "Drastheon is tiny."

Katrina snorted. "It is definitely *not* great," she said with a laugh. "Come on, Nocturne. Even you know that dumpy little town isn't anything to be proud of."

We both chuckled. An awkward silence ensued where we stared into each other's eyes. She looked away.

I had never met a human, not even one the non-cursed

elves, so brave amongst the druen. I liked that.

Our talking continued and my desire for her only strengthened. I had never felt this way a year prior for the cleaning-slave I thought I loved. I never felt that way for any of the flirtatious belles of Drastheon, however buxom and beautiful they thought they were. The feelings I had for Katrina were something much more.

That evening, after traveling five more miles in the ice cold snow, I found rest in the shade of an immense pine. The nettle-covered ground had been sheltered from the snow. The blizzard continued, and at night, the air dipped even colder.

Katrina, however, seemed have partially recovered. Color returned to her cheeks, and I think drinking the water and eating the haddock was working wonders, although we only had about four fish, now, between the two of us. We would have to conserve them over the coming days. I was no hunter, and even if I had been one, I had no bow.

As I held Katrina, I could feel her shivering. I knew how miserable both of us were: cold, fatigued, and out in the open. I wrapped the bearskin around both of us tight. I rubbed my arms against her. She loosened again, becoming gelatin in my arms.

She whispered, "Are you going to hurt me?"

"No," I whispered back.

Feeling her shivering as she sat in my lap was arousing me. I fought the crude feelings as hard as I could.

"Nocturne…"

"What?"

She turned around to face me. A wry smile crept over her lips. "What do you think of me?" she said.

"I think you're beautiful. I think you're brave and strong. I think you're smart. I think you're—"

She swallowed my words with her lips and didn't relinquish. I held her as we kissed, and my grip only tightened as it built momentum. All the feelings for me she hid were lavished upon me as the kissing turned to something far more: something animal and base, yet heartfelt.

The next morning, everything was different. She was the first girl I'd ever had; and I was her first as well. If I had my way, she would be my only one, too, like my father had long taught me.

We left a little late that morning.

"I'm not afraid of you anymore, Nocturne," Katrina said as we walked.

She sighed softly and nuzzled her head into my arms.

"You're no wolf. You're a sheep in wolf's clothing."

"I never thought of it that way," I said.

"Well that's what you are." Her lips were soft and wet, but the cold and blood loss had turned them bluish white. Poor, poor Katrina. She needed warmth and a plate of hot food. If only I could take her back to Drastheon—take her home to meet mother and father—perhaps marry her.

"I don't get it. Why are all the other vampires so cruel?"

"We grow up hating humans. And hating other elves, too, because they hate us. But I never bought into the rhetoric. You're just as smart, just as valuable as a—"

"I love you."

I withheld my shock. "I love you too, Katrina."

The next day we awoke a bit late for schedule, perhaps an hour after sunrise. As I stepped out of the shade of the cave to see the red-bronze horizon, I remembered all that had gone on. I knew I had fallen in love with Katrina, and that she had fallen in love with me.

I picked her up and carried her again in my arms. We talked of her past, and I listened keenly, not only because of my lack of knowledge of human lands but because I thought my interest in her had become far more than infatuation, far more serious than any fickle romance I'd had with any girls in Drastheon.

"I remember having fun back home," Katrina said. "In autumn we'd have the Apple Festival in Bandonshire, and one year I was voted the Apple Queen!"

"I'm not surprised, if it was a contest of beauty," I said.

"I'm sure you could've been the Apple King, if you weren't so white! Pale I don't mind, but you look like a corpse."

I grinned. "It is my natural skin tone, and that of all druen. I can't help it."

I was itching for shelter and wanted to give up the journey early. I was eager to relax, but spending days out here without food or water would mean certain death and we needed to get to a village.

We stopped at dusk. The hindrance of snow and cold made it impossible to travel more than ten miles in the day. I suspected that it would be a long time before we found any form of settlement. I knew that my hometown, Drastheon, was in southern section of Nardur, but I did not know which direction the stream was leading us; north, south, or every direction at once.

We continued following the stream and as we walked, we talked whenever we could.

I learned much about Katrina Stanbridge, how her family owned the most famous vineyard in the region of Bandonshire, of her mother and father and how it made her cry when she thought of how worried they must be. She begged me to reassure her that I would take her back to see her parents. I did, and I hoped my promises would hold true.

From what Katrina told me of human culture it sounded much kinder, more expressive and more hospitable than cold, uncaring druenic culture. I was amazed to hear her great love for her parents, though I knew it was unlikely that all humans are as wonderful as she.

On the third evening the stream dried up. My first instinct was to panic. But I kept my calm, since I was in charge.

I could see rocky, jutting hills in the distance. No trees covered them, only snow and tufts of brownish grass. To the side, perhaps a half-mile out, I could see the stormy gray Eastern Sea. Then I realized we had been traveling almost directly south—we were at the border of the land of Sardur.

Sardur was the home of a strange folk of whom various and conflicting accounts had reached my ears. They were called the *Quilloren Somnaren*—the Elf Eaters—or Hill Ghouls. They, like we Narduren, were descended from our ancestor, Prince Gilden. They were slightly more bestial, however, and given over to their bloodlust, like the Morthen of Nardur. But they had one civilized town—Gal Arion—and if I could find that, then perhaps food, mead and comfort would not be far away. From there, we could move even further southward, to the kingdom of the non-cursed elves, the kingdom of Londor and the legendary castles of East Arlom.

"Nocturne?" Katrina said in a voice slightly stronger than usual.

"Yes, dear?" I asked.

"Are we going there, to those hills?" Her eyes bore into me. "I have a bad feeling. I just have a bad feeling about them. The thought of going there makes me numb."

"We are going," I said sternly. "And you shouldn't feel bad at all, because I will protect you."

"Let's go somewhere," she said. "Let's spend time one more night together before we die."

"We are not going to die," I repeated firmly.

But I honored her wishes just the same.

CHAPTER THREE: THE HILL CANNIBALS

We rose from our sleeping places in the shelter of the rock-hills, and prepared to begin our journey. I woke Katrina and she stirred from her sleep. Her eyes were glazed and shallow in that way that can only mean dread.

"I'm scared," she whispered. "I'm just really scared, Nocturne… sometimes you have to trust your feelings."

"Feelings mean nothing," I told her.

"It's intuition," she explained.

"That's ridiculous. Sardur is the quickest way back to your parents."

"Yes, but Nocturne, won't you listen to me?" she said. A tear began to form. "Haven't you ever been scared before?"

"Yes," I said. "But never about an irrational feeling."

She sniffed and then wiped the tear away. "Let's go."

We filled our stomachs with the last of the salted haddock, drank from a nearby spring until our thirsts were sated, and started scaling the towering hills that bordered Sardur. Katrina was healthy enough to walk, even to climb with help. As we scaled the jagged gray stone, I reassured her. But when she finally conceded and changed her outlook, it was more an acceptance of her fate than an overcoming of her irrational feelings.

As I walked I could hear the rolling thrush of the waves far in the distance, and hear the seagulls squawking and flying through the chilly air. The coastal scene was so tranquil, so serene. The sky was cloudless and bright blue. The sun had begun to gently melt away the six inches of snow that had accumulated. Winter was giving way to the year's thaw, and back in Drastheon the village people were probably relaxing on verandas with tall mugs of mead and baked crab legs. One has to take advantage of good weather in druen lands, for there, Mother Nature is never kind for long.

Panting, thighs burning, stopping only occasionally to drink water, we scaled the rock-hills. An hour later we came to the crest of the miniature mountains. We had done it. Doubtlessly they deterred most travelers from entering here, but I knew it was the safest path. Below us, the hills descended into a bumpy, rocky land covered in dead brown grass, tumbleweeds and shrubs.

So far, I saw no ghouls or anything living thing. The hills of Sardur were completely empty.

"Look around you," I told her, motioning to the barren landscape. "The hills of Sardur are as empty as the arctic wastes. No bears or rabbits or reindeer, not a living soul. And soon we'll find Gal Arion and be on our way to your parents!"

Her eyes glinted as she spoke. "Soon we will get to the River Galios." We could take a boat downriver. I *will* see my parents again. Oh, gods…"

I put my arm around her and embraced her. Then we continued down through the barren hills.

The country of the Hill Ghouls was a frozen rock plateau where nothing but tufts of grass could grow. There were a handful of pines, but these were spread out very far. Certainly, out of the two druen tribes, the Sarduren had drawn the shortest straw. No lumber, precious little game and certainly no agriculture.

The sun was setting as Katrina and I walked along. The total silence of the rocky land was at first comforting, but as night set in, and I could hear nothing but our footsteps, it became something eerie. Color seeped from the sky, an unsettled feeling came over me and I grew jittery. Occasionally there were faint rustlings which I told Katrina were only tumbleweeds. But there was no wind.

Still, I saw nothing.

Then I did. Something—no, *someone*—was perched upon a hill looking at us. The thing was druen and humanoid in form; two legs, two arms, and a head. But he drooled, his eyes were wide, his fangs were visible. He was completely naked, which revealed a repulsively thin form. His skin stretched tight across his protruding bones. His fangs were extended and his fingernails had grown very long. He was a druen who had given in to Gilden's Curse; he was a druen gone mad.

The beast screeched at the top of his lungs and more of his friends emerged over the hills—naked, hunchbacked, and bald. They truly were the sons of the night.

Screaming, they dashed toward us with claws extended.

"Wagh!" one screamed. "Fresh meat! Rip skin from bones! Fill guts with blood!"

"Boy mine!"

"Girl mine!"

As the screams echoed across the rocky plateau, I drew my knife: the only weapon I had. My heart was pounding out of control. My blood had turned to ice. Katrina was crying.

"I told you!" she wept. "I told you."

"I'll protect you!" I said, though I did not believe it.

Soon the Hill Cannibals had surrounded us, gnashing their teeth. Their desire for our blood was nothing if not insane. There was nothing in this world they wanted more than to open our veins and drink deep.

One leapt for me and I cut open his throat. Another

charged but I grabbed his shoulders and sank my teeth deep into his flesh. As the arousing blood gave me a slight high—slight because his blood was second-hand—I forced myself to wrench away and stab another Hill Ghoul through his bony chest. But there were far too many for me to handle.

The stars were out now, and the ghouls approached in droves, although they seemed afraid of my knife and did not have weapons themselves; apparently the Hill Ghouls had gone so mad with bloodlust that they no longer remembered how to use tools.

I was shaking. Katrina's knees were buckled. "I told you," she said. "Hell! I told you."

"Back, savages!" I screamed and swept my knife at them hard and fast. But the night was young and even more ghouls appeared over the rocky hills of Sardur. They would rather have died than missed out on a bloodmeal.

I should have listened to Katrina, no matter how foolish her feelings had seemed. But there was no point in wishing or hoping things were different, there was only time to try and save ourselves.

Katrina howled in fright. A ghoul grabbed her with a bony hand and wrenched her into the crowd of monsters.

I let out a wail. *"Katrina!"* I dashed to her but it was no use.

With the loss of her life, I found myself suddenly unconcerned about my own. I struck down perhaps two more before one of them slashed my arm with a claw. And the puncture went deep, opening my veins. It was only seconds before my arms were covered in the warm, red liquid that the ghouls wanted so badly. Their tongues lolled hungrily as they climbed over each other for the first hit.

I managed to cut open one last ghoul's throat before a large, muscular one clawed me in the back. The blow knocked the wind out of my lungs and I stumbled forward, trying as hard as I could to fight them off.

But the ghouls had overwhelmed me, and when another monster's fist pounded hard into my skull, I made a conscious decision to give up my life.

CHAPTER FOUR: DANDRINNAS

The first thing I realized when I awoke was that I was warm, very warm. I was covered in something very soft: furs. A blanket of bearskins and beaver pelts. I was sitting on a wicker chair in a wooden hut, my feet propped near a blazing hearth.

The second thing I realized was that, to my great surprise, I was alive. And the next thing I remembered made that thought not wholly pleasant.

"I have such a bad feeling about this place."

"I told you!"

"Nocturne, help!"

Katrina had died. My throat moistened and I let loose. I buried my head in my hands and wept like I never had before, crying into the blanket. What horrid fate had Katrina had met? Had she been picked apart and eaten alive? Or had she been dragged away to a cave somewhere and tormented, then sucked dry?

Either way she was dead, and it was my fault.

The sobbing ended eventually. My internal reservoir of tears had dried. Only then did I have the peace of mind to wonder how I had gotten here.

An elven man approached me. He was doubtlessly druen, with pasty white skin and even whiter hair. He wore a dull brown robe woven with black lace. His face was old and wrinkled, but wise.

"You are awake," he said in a low, resonant voice. "You've been unconscious for days. The Hill Cannibals drank half your blood."

My stomach churned. "Where are we?" I said.

The man smiled and looked on me with calm eyes. He appeared to be getting on in age, but he looked healthy. He sat down on a wicker chair close to mine.

"We are still in Sardur," he said. "I saved you from the Mad Ones. You are in my hut on a hill which they are afraid to approach."

"What is your name?" I said.

"Aldor," he said. In his hand he held a bowl filled with greasy broth. He lifted the spoon to my lips.

In my weak and thin state, the broth was a magic elixir. It was fatty, salty, and spiced with herbs.

"What is your name, boy?"

"Nocturne. Are the Hill Ghouls after us?" Aldor shook his head. "The Mad Ones know very well not to approach this hill; they flee from my sight. I am their greatest fear; I am a Sane One."

"What is a Narduren doing here? Why did you leave our home?"

"I am one of the Sarduren," he said, smiling. "Of the ones you call Hill Cannibals."

"But how could you be? You're not like them. You're wearing clothing!"

"Once I was mad, like the ones who killed you," Aldor said, offering me some more broth, "but that is too much for you to think about right now. So don't think. Just relax, and eat your soup."

I leaned back in my chair, noticing how radically different Aldor was from the ghouls. A pinewood bookshelf sat near the doorway, piled with thick, rolled-up parchment scrolls and vellum codices.

"Where did you get those books in such a barbaric place?" I asked, pointing to the books.

"After the city of Gal Arion went mad, I took these documents from the old library."

"Gal Arion went mad?"

Aldor nodded. "It is inevitable as a druen—with a city like Gal Arion, a beacon of reason in a land of insanity—to give in to the vampire's most maddening and unclean passion: bloodlust. Natural decay. Societal rot. Gal Arion fell because of it."

"So it's not there anymore?"

Aldor shook his head. "The people of Gal Arion went mad one night five years past. Only ruins remain. Come now, finish your soup or go to sleep."

I chose the latter. Heavy sleep came within seconds of shutting my eyes.

I awoke early in the morning and saw the blue sky through the open tent-flap. I pulled the fur blanket tighter and rolled over. We were near the stormy waters of the Eastern Sea, and over the great silver ocean the sun was rising.

Aldor sat across from me at his chair, his hands neatly folded over his lap. His staff leaned against the wall, near the door that led outside. I had the chilling feeling that he had just been sitting there, watching me, for hours.

"I have great faith in you, that you will recover," Aldor said when he noticed I had awoken. "I have great faith that you will emerge from your sickness a better druen, or no longer a druen at all."

I raised a brow.

"You are a blood drinker, are you not?" he continued, his voice cool and crisp. "The smell of blood lingers over you like a cloud."

"Aren't we all blood drinkers?" I said. I could hear a pot simmering in the hearth.

Aldor's brows furrowed. "Have you ever heard of the Oath

of Dandrinnas?"

I shook my head slowly.

"Did you know that the curse of Gilden—that wretched lord of evil—can be undone?"

"Gilden was not good, but he is our ancestor and it is wrong to speak ill of him." I sat up to elucidate my point, but a wave of nausea overcame over me. "The patriarch of the druen race is not to be scorned or despised. Even you, Aldor, are born of him!"

"Born of him, but not of his spirit."

"Bullocks."

"Do you worship the patriarch of the druen, whose evil was unmatched across the world?"

"Worship him?" I sneered. "No. Give him due respect? Yes."

"Then we disagree," Aldor said, smiling darkly. "And you may have your opinion, no matter how wrong it may be. You have your free will. But we have digressed. I wish to speak of something called the Oath of Dandrinnas." His eyes glistened. "It is how I overcame the slavering madness of the ghouls—how I, one of the Sarduren, became civilized. How I turned from wild beast into a thinker and—some might argue—a true elf. I abandoned the drinking of sentient blood totally."

"Everyone slips up once in a while. Everyone drinks blood. People don't like to talk about it, perhaps, but everyone does it."

"Certain animals—deer, moose, cows and other beasts—can give the minimal nourishment required to get through each day cleanly. Although it isn't as satisfying as drinking from a human or an elf's veins, it does take the desire away sans pleasure. And it is a clean act. It may be hard at first. But after a year or so, it isn't so much a struggle."

"Ridiculous," I said. "Why would you subject yourself to

such torture?"

Aldor smiled. "To be able to say, 'I have beat the Curse.' I have defeated madness with sanity. I am not a ghoul; I am a true druen."

I sneered and tried to get off the chair again. My body wouldn't permit it. "Take me south to the border of Sardur. I don't plan on staying in this frozen hunk of rock for much longer."

"The Hill Cannibals will smell the blood on you. You have drunk from someone's veins recently; even I can tell. We must wait a week, before the scent wears off, before I can take you to the edge of Londor."

I nodded slowly. The Kingdom of Londor was civilized. I had never been to non-druen lands before in my life—I had never really strayed that far from Drastheon before, until now.

But I could not go back to Nardur; I had betrayed my race for a human, and in vampire lands that was an unforgettable transgression.

I awoke late the next morning and after I had stirred around a while, Aldor came into the room to attend to me. He had a bowl in his hand, but this time the hot, salty brown broth was mixed with vegetables and scraps of meat. Taking the bowl and a spoon, I started to devour it hungrily.

"Whom have you been crying for?" Aldor said.

I had been distracted from Katrina's death, staying here. I said her name.

"The girl you were traveling with?" Aldor asked. "Was she your lover?"

I nodded slowly. "She was," I said.

"She is at peace now."

I set my spoon down. "How do you know?" I said. "How

do you know anything awaits us beyond this life?"

Aldor sighed. "I only wished to comfort you, Nocturne."

"I do not believe in the gods."

"So you think she is only rotting, food for the maggots?"

"I don't know."

"Well, I hope one day you will find a better way to console yourself."

"Did you see her die?" I asked between bites. "Did you see what happened to her?"

Aldor shook his head. "They dragged her away; I didn't see what happened to her. But she did not survive. The Mad Ones do not leave survivors."

I looked away and stared out the window toward the sea. The gulls were soaring above the beach and I could smell sea salt in the air.

One cold morning, we were both slumped over hot mugs of tea. Our discussion turned to our shared heritage, to the race of druen.

"How much do you know about our forefather, Prince Gilden?" he said.

I took a sip of the steaming drink and set it back on the table. "He was unkind," I said simply. "But he is my ancestor, and I will not dishonor him."

"He went far beyond unkind," Aldor said. "Would you like to hear the full, unabridged story, Nocturne?"

I sat back in the chair. "Humor me."

"Prince Gilden was the son of the king of the Lamen Elves," Aldor said, "King Danthemari the Ninth, to be specific. And as Gilden was growing into a man, Danthemari noticed his son was a bit different from the other children. The signs of his evil began at an early age. His sister, Elloré, became an object of desire for him. He lusted after her, and Elloré was equally perverse. In fact, she welcomed his unnatural desire for her. One day his father found them sleeping in the same bed, and filled with anger, he nearly sent Gilden to exile. But he did not cut off the problem. He did not sentence his son to death.

"And even stupider and more oblivious was the king, in hindsight. A few years later he proclaimed his son Gilden the prefect of Londor, and he was given the throne over the province to rule the city of Marlon. He ruled there for many years—with an exceptionally cruel fist, I might add. The people of Marlon called him Gilden the Impaler. Indeed, he made a gruesome spectacle of anyone who opposed him—you name the device of foul torture, he surely used it. And it was there in Marlon that he officially married his sister, Elloré, and she gave birth to Sarsoli, ancestor of Sardur. With a chambermaid he had the son Narsoli—ancestor of *your* people.

"In the early years of the War of Shadow, he sided with the lord of evil, Seymus. He attempted to depose the gods from their thrones in Heaven. He made war on his father Danthemari; he declared Londor a separate kingdom. And it was during the war that he performed the cruelest of acts. One of his generals rebelled against him, thinking that Gilden was a maniac. And do you know what he did? He served the body of General Dankari to the people of Marlon… as food for the winter solstice celebration. But his depravity did not end there. When the war was over and the forces of good had overcome the lord of darkness, he was unsatisfied with his station in life. He declared himself the god of the earth, and he declared his wife and sister Elloré the goddess of sun and moon. And according to the ancient elvish creation myth—the one before the discovery of the true gods—the Terrestrial God killed his sister, the Celestial Goddess. He killed Elloré with his own hands."

I looked at him in surprise.

"And then, seeing this great darkness, the High God cursed Gilden's descendants forevermore to hunger for the blood of men. Then came the Black Night, when the wild sons of Sarsoli chased the citizens of Marlon through the streets, struck them down and drank their blood. The next day the children of Gilden were chased by the other elves far away, into the frigid northern wastes, to live forever shrouded in the darkness and cold. Sarsoli and his wild sons settled in Sardur, and Narsoli settled in Nardur. And you are the son of Narsoli; furthermore, you are a son of Gilden. And if you do not overcome the bloodlust like I want you to, then you carry his evil."

I set my teacup down and looked at Aldor contemptuously. I did not like him; I did not believe him, either. But arguing with him would be pointless, and I had better ways to spend my time.

The next morning Aldor and I left the hut. We wandered through the barren hills where nothing but shrubs and moss grew. By day Sardur was a safe place, without ghouls; they did not emerge except in darkness. They slept in their caves by day and emerged by night to drink the blood of men.

We found a perch on a rocky cliff and waited. Aldor had given me a bow, and all I suspected we were doing was hunting to get more venison for his stews. But I was wrong.

Eventually, after hours of waiting, an elk came into the valley below. How majestic were they with their great antlers, and how gracefully they walked; with what fury did the hunters slay them.

Slowly, Aldor raised his bow and knocked a goose feathered arrow to the string. "Now do as I say," the old man whispered as he took aim. He released the arrow into the air and it struck the elk's gut. It hobbled away at a pathetic speed.

"Run after it, and drink from its veins," Aldor whispered urgently. "Then you will understand Dandrinnas."

I chased the elk over hills and hills and through deep dales and valleys, past shrubs and open barrens covered in moss and lichen. Eventually it could run no more and collapsed. I leapt onto it. My druen muscles were strong, and I aimed well.

I felt slight sorrow as I sank my teeth deep into its neck, as I felt the blood rush into my gums. The high was nonexistent—I felt no pleasure—but just as Aldor said the blood satisfied me and took away the urge and desire. I drank and drank for several minutes before the blood was all dried up. Then I stood up, feeling my fangs retract, and took a deep breath.

Aldor came up behind me. He had been running behind me, a few hundred feet away. He made the distance in good time. "Good work, Nocturne," he hollered.

I smiled and looked at my teacher. I felt good. I felt clean. I had begun my journey to overcome the Curse; I had begun my journey down the path of Dandrinnas. There was no guilt; the desire was gone, but I felt virtuous.

And in that instant I realized why Aldor prided himself on being able to say, "The gods cannot turn me into a monster. I am an elf. I am not a druen. I am not a son of Gilden."

The nourishment sentient blood gave me, I decided, wasn't worth the shame and the guilt that followed quickly on its heels. I was better than that. I was better than the Morthen, and I was better than the beasts of Sardur.

CHAPTER FIVE: NOCTURNE DANDRINNASSI

The summer months came upon the land. The snows melted, paving new streams through the frozen rock of Sardur. Purple wildflowers had bloomed on the sides of the brown hills, and it was beautiful again.

In between bites of my venison stew, I asked Aldor, "Am I ready to go? Am I ready to live amongst the True Elves?"

"No. You must learn to defend yourself, Nocturne," he continued, "You must learn to fight those who would harm you."

"I can defend myself well enough."

"The fact that I had to rescue you indicates otherwise," said Aldor. "Today—and every day from hereon—we practice swordplay. Soon, you will become a master of the blade like I am. Then, and only then, will I allow you to go."

"What will I practice with?" I said.

He got up from his chair and disappeared into the other room for perhaps a minute. When he finally returned he had a pair of daggers in his hand—glistening weapons with sharp steel blades, and elegant leather-lined handles. The pommels were glazed with silver and gold. "These are yours now," Aldor said. "They once belonged to an unfortunate victim of the ghouls, whom I was not able to save. Name them what you will. They are yours now, Nocturne."

I eyed one. "*Dreské*," I said. I held up the other and said, "*Draské*."

"Ah, the two fangs of the dragon Noruggi," Aldor said with a smile. "Your classical references show fine taste."

I smiled. After grabbing the daggers, we walked outside to practice. We sparred with the weapons, careful not to draw blood.

A few weeks passed. My grief for Katrina did not totally cease, but it did dull. Sometimes I went long periods without thinking of her, where I thought about the present and not on the past.

One evening as the sun was setting, I had begun searching through the stony hills for game. I needed to sate my lust for blood in a clean and civilized manner, as Aldor had long taught me. But though I had spent the day watching from my hunting spot, I had yet to see or hear anything living in these hills—no elk or deer chewing at the tufts of grass. I sighed and turned back towards Aldor's hut. I would go without drinking blood tonight. I planned on trying again tomorrow.

But I had been paying too much attention to the hunt. The sky was darkening and I was beginning to get a bit worried that I would not make it back before nightfall.

By the time I had made it halfway, the sun had set. I could see Aldor's hut far in the distance. The jabbering of ghouls echoed across the hills as they stirred from their nests in Sardur's dank caverns. I supposed the dagger-skills I had been practicing would be put to the test. But not if I could help it. Immediately I began sprinting towards the Hill.

As I ran the ghouls' jabbers turned to howls. I was about a minute away, sprinting toward the safety of the hut, when a crazed ghoul came leaping from a nearby crevice. He barred his fangs in front of me and took a swipe at my face with its bony fingers. I backed away and swept the daggers from their sheaths.

I charged the ghoul and punched *Dreské* cleanly through its shoulder, then slit his throat with *Dreské*. Blood poured from both wounds as I followed them up with a hard sidewise cleave, and decapitated him cleanly. The ghoul sank to the cold, mossy ground in a pile of black blood.

I started sprinting again. I heard quick footsteps behind me, getting closer and closer. I tried as hard as I could to run faster, but I was going at full capacity, and before I had made it to Aldor's hill the ghouls surrounded me.

"I get his blood!" one hissed.

"No, me get his blood!"

"*Blood!*" one of them howled at the top of his lungs. At the cue several other crazed screams of *"Blood!"* echoed through the night air.

"Back, sons of Gilden!" I shouted and charged at the one in front, striking and missing with *Dreské.* I whipped around and made a feeble cut at another. But one of the ghouls grasped a hold of me. His fangs touched my neck.

I writhed and threw him off me with all my might. Now the Monsters were within inches of me and ready to do whatever it took to drink my blood.

I slashed in a fury, cutting down three ghouls in the span of seconds. But I knew they were too close and soon I would be done in.

Miraculously, it seemed to me, I broke through their grasp and sprinted as fast as I could up the hill to Aldor's hut. But the ghouls hopped along quickly in pursuit.

A ghoul running far ahead of the pack leapt for me, grabbed my leg and tripped me, and started pulling me backwards. I screamed and struggled to get back up, but it was no use. I wondered whether I was going to die.

Then, just as the ravenous ghouls were ready to make a feast of me, the door of Aldor's hut flew open. He dashed out and held up his staff at the ghouls. They screamed.

"Old man!"

"Run 'way!"

They fled.

I got to my feet and up the hill, panting.

"You have grown skillful, to fend them off," Aldor said. "Skillful, but lucky. You still have much to learn."

Over the ensuing weeks, we sparred and practiced fighting techniques, cuts, parries, and dodges. On the last day of summer, I defeated Aldor in a sparring match.

Over that period, the Oath of Dandrinnas became vital and sacred to me. Every month or so, when I was consumed by desire, I spent the day hunting for deer or elk, wounded them with an arrow, and drank from their veins until my bloodlust was satisfied. Then I would drag home the carcass, and Aldor would skin it and dress it and butcher it, and make stew.

One time in the coolness of the evening, as Aldor and I reclined in the living room with cups of tea and books in both our hands, he said something very surprising.

"I feel I have done what I needed to," he said. "You have learned the path of Dandrinnas; I have made a new convert. In my time I have made four; and I plan on converting more. I think it is time you head south for Londor, like you wanted to."

"Do you really think I am ready to assimilate with non-druen, Aldor?"

"I think you are more than ready," Aldor said. "I think you will grow idle and self-satisfied if you stay here in the comfort of my hut. You must go live amongst the True Elves, now."

"I agree," I said, "but I don't know the way."

"We will go south," he said. "Straight south. Past the mountainous border is a trickling stream that divides Sardur and East Arlom. That's where I'll leave you. Eventually you will come to some sort of settlement, a farm or town. You can ask directions there." He looked into my eyes. "Now Nocturne, I want you to go to the city of Naremon. I have a friend there who takes in recovering druen. His name is Parthori Tana. He lives on 11 Mymar Street, in the Lower City. Can you remember that?"

"Yes."

"We will leave together tomorrow morning—the journey is forty miles but we are not going to stop until we get there. It may be tiring, but the ghouls will give us trouble if we don't continue full-force ahead. Understood?"

I nodded, thinking to myself that I would miss the gentle relaxation of Aldor's hut, the quiet afternoons of hot tea and books, the warmth of the fire and the companionship of a sane, docile druen.

The journey was easier without the snow and the icy blasts of the North Wind. We walked from dawn until well into the night, until my legs throbbed and burned. We came to the steep hills that surrounded Sardur.

We scaled them with a bit of difficulty. By then my legs were sore and aching, but I wanted to get out of Sardur as fast as I could. I climbed quickly to the peak. I saw a trickling stream at the bottom, then a flat, grassy plain that stretched as far as I could see.

Aldor's laid his hand on my shoulder. "I am proud of you, Nocturne," he said. "Let no one call you a bloodsucker. Let no one call you a vampire, or a son of Gilden."

"I am a son of Gilden," I said.

"Perhaps in flesh, but not in spirit," Aldor said. "You will live amongst the True Elves from now until the day you die."

"I hope so."

Aldor took out a pouch of silver coins. "This is elven money," he said. "Use it to buy your way to Naremon. Go there and prosper. Meet Parthori Tana on Mymar Street, in the Lower City. He will take you in, Nocturne."

I nodded and smiled. "Thank you, Aldor, for teaching me so much."

He smiled.

"I will leave you now, Aldor."

"Farewell, Nocturne Dandrinnassi."

CHAPTER SIX: PARTHORI TANA

Daggers buckled at my side, I stood at the doorstep of 11 Mymar Street in the pouring rain. Parthori lived in an upper room.

I had traveled through the Great North Plain for three weeks and arrived at the town of Don, inquired for directions and took the road from there, staying at inns along the way. After a two-week journey, I had arrived at the gate to the Lower City of Naremon.

Naremon's architecture was elegant. The roofs were triangular, slightly curved, and tiled with bright purple shingles. The windows were almost always of pure glass. This was nothing like the huts and wooden houses of Nardur; it was as if everyone lived in miniature mansions. Multistoried mansions that were sometimes quite tall, but never unwieldy.

Naremon was divided into two cities: the aristocratic Upper and the commoners' Lower. The Lower City existed in a valley beneath the Upper. Parthori's flat sat in a rather prosperous section of the Lower City, and it had taken me hours to find it. The people of Naremon did not help very much; none seem especially interested in my plight or my foreign accent. They did not care to respond when I approached them.

I entered the first floor of 11 Mymara Street and found myself at a cobbler's shop. I stomped my wet boots on the rug and shook the ice-cold rain off my cloak. Inside was the shopkeeper, a very old man perhaps in his 200s.

"How do I get to Parthori Tana from here?" I asked.

"Thori lives upstairs," the cobbler says. "Third story. Two flights of stairs, 'n you'll find 'im."

I nodded and followed his instructions.

The stairs were rather creaky and old, and the whole place smelled of old dust, but I struggled through it and made it to the door.

Parthori answered a few moments after I had knocked. He had long, graying black hair tied in a ponytail and a ruddy face. He was getting on in years: a hundred or so, perhaps. His dark green eyes were the color of grass in summer. He wore a tunic, over which he had pulled a stitched leather vest. He said, "Greetings."

"Greetings," I replied.

"And you are?"

"Nocturne," I said. "Nocturne Rabaam."

"What can I do for you?"

"Aldor sent me."

Parthori smiled and opened the door a crack wider. "Come inside."

His apartment was rather small, the size of my bedroom back in Nardur. I wondered how a person could live here.

"Go warm yourself by the fire," he continued, "I can't stand to see you wet and cold. I've some porridge cooking in the pot. Is that all right with you?"

"Porridge is fine," I said, shivering.

He removed my coat and placed it on the rack near the door. He gave me a disapproving look, as if I should have known to do such a thing; but I quite honestly didn't care. Then Parthori led me to the couch, and I sat down and rubbed my hands in the flaring warmth of the fireplace.

Parthori returned with two bowls and two wooden spoons.

"I believe the porridge is ready," he said. Taking the iron ladle that was already in the pot, he scooped the hot, whitish mush into a bowl and handed it to me. Then he repeated the same process for himself, and sat down beside me.

"Nothing like hot porridge on a cold day," Parthori said with a smile.

I smiled and nodded, shoveling down the tasteless mush down as quickly as I could. It was rather hot and warmed my frigid bones; and it took the edge off my hunger, though I knew I'd be starving two hours later.

"Now, Nocturne, let's talk about what we are going to do with you."

"I'd love to hear it," I said.

"There is an inn on this street, the Waning Crescent Inn, famous for its great food and atmosphere. People even come from the Upper City to dine there."

"Are you trying to advertise? I don't have much money to spare."

He chuckled. "I see that you have a sense of humor." He smiled. "Now the Waning Crescent Inn may appear normal—served by a team of friendly elves. But those friendly elves are actually vampires who are working together to overcome their bloodlust. They all share the same last name, as you do: Dandrinnassi."

"My family name is Rabaam."

He glared. "You are a follower of Dandrinnas, and you forego your druenic surname."

In my mind I knew I would never do such a thing—I was the son of Drethori Rabaam, forever—but I kept my lips shut.

"The leader is a man who has become one with the spirit of Dandrinnas. His name is Sildé Dandrinnassi and will instruct you how to make a good living and be a productive member of society amongst the True Elves. There are two rules."

"What?"

"Do not speak the word 'druen' aloud lest Queen Madiré's

men overhear you. It is not legal for us to live amongst the citizens. The second, never commiserate about your bloodlust even among your friends. This breeds desire even more. It can lead to a breech in conduct and is ultimately counterproductive." He paused, setting his finished bowl of porridge on the table. "Ten druen work at the Waning Crescent Inn. Now, with you, there are eleven. You must support each other, and drive the thought of drinking blood far from your mind."

I was beginning to dislike Parthori for his superior attitude. Something about his tone seemed to suggest I was inferior to him because I was less accomplished in the Path. But I kept silent. Working at the inn would at least produce a decent living, and I could break either of the two rules he had spouted, as long as no one discovered me.

The rain was splashing hard on the shingled roof of the building and the fire did not completely suffice to warm me.

The silence was broken by Parthori's voice.

"Try hard. Try ever so hard to purge the very fleeting thought of blood from your mind. The druen who give in to their lusts are inferior to us. They are animals; they are the sons of Gilden. Beasts. Now try so very hard, and perhaps, one day, you will become like me."

I repressed a glare. But I consoled myself with the fact that Parthori would not be working at the Waning Crescent. Perhaps the druen there would be a bit more compassionate.

Perhaps some of them would reach down from lofty heights to touch such a lowly, pitiful being such as I. I laughed quietly to myself.

CHAPTER SEVEN: HOMAR DRUENON

The Waning Crescent was a spacious establishment, three stories tall, far larger than the pathetically tiny hut of an inn at Drastheon. The roof was elaborate and shingled with luminous purple tiles, and in the courtyard in front was a fountain spraying water up into the air. The walls were painted clear stark white, and every window was of colored glass.

I entered the lobby without further delay.

A sizeable group of customers had gathered in the lobby, and all tribes of elves seemed to be represented; four golden-haired Lamen, nine black-haired Lonen, and one brown-haired Umen. All tribes except the ignoble Kardir Tribe that is, who spent their barbaric lives wandering the land on a never-ending and purposeless hunt. Survival was the whole purpose of their existence; therefore, their existence was justified by nothing, and some scholars logically concluded that their survival was not important, even counterproductive.

A black-haired elf approached me quickly. "How can I help you, good sire?" he said. "I am the innkeeper, Sildé."

"Sildé Dandrinnassi?" I said quiet enough that no one could hear, and grinned.

His eyes bulged. "Fool. Get in the kitchen and I'll explain your duties."

He met me inside the inn's tiny kitchen where one of the workers was dicing carrots. Beside him were several slabs of chicken and a plethora of vegetables, and behind that stood a huge lead cauldron boiled underneath a burning fire.

"Don't pull a fool joke like that again," Sildé hissed. "Now we don't have room for you. You are going to room with Homar here." He looked back. "Homar, introduce yourself!"

The person cooking turned to greet me. He was young like me, thirty or thirty-five perhaps, handsome and stylishly dressed. His black hair was cut a bit shorter than mine, so that it was almost a shave, and his eyes were dark brown in contrast to my blue. "What's your name?" he asked.

"Nocturne," I said.

"I'm Homar. Homar Druenon," he answered.

"Homar Dandrinnassi," Sildé corrected him poisonously.

I smiled. Perhaps I would get to like Homar, after all.

The rest of the day was spent chopping carrots, slicing onions, skinning potatoes, dicing raw chicken and combining all those elements into a steaming cauldron to make soup for dinner. The stew was seasoned with salt and pepper and thyme and rosemary, and when it had reached a certain thickness we started ladling it into wooden bowls for the inn patrons. By the end of the night half was still left, so we saved it for breakfast.

When our tasks were done, and all I wanted to do was put my frigid, exhausted body into a soft warm bed, Sildé announced that our workday was finished. We got a feathered mattress from the storage room and placed it in Homar's chamber.

That night, as we lay in our beds, we talked of our families, of our past in the now-distant land of Nardur.

"The House Druenon is quite prominent in Agnon City," Homar said.

"Where is that? I think I've heard of it."

"It's quite close to the capital. About a three-mile ride north along the river from Druenel Hai. Population of a thousand, last census—decent size I'd say."

"And what brought you here?"

"A man preaching about Dandrinnas came to Agnon City one day, and I'd seen what bloodlust can do to a druen, how mad a person can be driven by it. The philosophy sat well with me. So I talked to him that night… he told me to flee the land of temptation and come here, to Naremon. I did. The journey was long, but worth it."

I nodded. Then I relayed to him the story of the ghouls, of Katrina, how the woman I had loved died because I did not listen to her intuition.

"No offense, Nocturne, but that's really foolish, going into Sardur unprepared," Homar said. "Going to Sardur at all is idiotic!"

"I didn't think things through," I told him. "And I didn't know it was *that* deadly to travel there."

"The Hill Ghouls are monsters. At least we Narduren have civilization."

We lay in silence for a minute or so. Then Homar spoke.

"Well, the women here are very pretty," he said simply. "Very pretty. And a brothel on every corner. In fact, I know of one in our neighborhood, *the Succubus Den*, with excellent pricing, and exquisite service. I'm sure you'll find someone like Katrina, if you look hard enough."

"I doubt it," I said. "I will never find another like her. It may sound immoral but I found her mortality, her frailness, her—humanity—alluring. She was strong and willful."

"Well the women here are strong, but they can be a bit domineering," Homar said. "This one gal, Yanré her name was, demanded that I clean up the table after we had dinner while she relaxed on the couch!"

"No one will ever replace Katrina," I said.

"Well, perhaps you're right. But I think it is time for me to go to."

"Good night," I said.

CHAPTER EIGHT: THE AMPHITHEATRE

For the next week I worked at the inn, cooking the dishes that Sildé wanted—chicken stew, beef stew, roast lamb and more—and then serving them to guests. Homar was always a great help, but the work was still tiring, and I wanted to go explore the city.

So on Saturday, when both Homar and I had a break, we did just that. Together we purchased seats at the Amphitheater of Draanon a few city blocks in the distance. A ticket only cost one silver, and I was confident the show would be greatly entertaining. But when we got to the doorstep, I noticed the guards were not elves at all, nor were they human slaves.

They were skeletons dressed up in armor, standing upright, with blue fire burning in their eye sockets. A chill ran up my spine.

I stopped a few feet away from them, only staring at them.

"Don't worry," Homar reassured me, gently brushing my back and propelling me forward. "They are controlled by the court necromancers. They conjure up the dead to serve the queen as guards, but as long as you don't do anything illegal they won't hurt you."

I soon realized the reason for our cheap tickets: the seats were close to the top of the Amphitheater. Within minutes of settling down, the trumpets pealed and the games began. It was difficult to see all that was going on, but I could make out the form of a human gladiator, barrel-chested and stark naked except for a helmet, fending off a pack of wolves with a trident and a net. He fought superbly well, parrying the snips of the ravenous wolves—who'd obviously been starved before the games—with exceptional grace and speed. Every time a wolf fell dead, the crowd erupted into a deafening cheer.

"He is one of the stars of the Arena," Homar said. "His name is Rhyon. That's not his real name but it's the name the elves gave him when he became a slave."

Rhionas was proclaimed victor over the wolves and a wreath of pine boughs was placed on his head. Then he was escorted by two purple-robed men through one of the Arena's iron gates.

As I looked around, I saw the queen of Naremon in the royal box with her handmaidens. She was quite close by, actually, a few seats down, but her box was protected with an iron fence. The queen herself was thin, with a plain face and a shapely physique that didn't quite compensate, and thick, ruffled black hair. A large golden crown studded with gems sat upon her head. She sat on a cushioned throne, and she seemed to be enjoying the games greatly. Every time a man or beast died, she stood up and cheered; something I found rather repulsive. But perhaps it was just my conservative tastes.

Next, a group of twenty human slaves with light skin were let out of the west gate, and a group of twenty human slaves with black skin were let out of the east gate. Each held a spear and leather shield in his hand.

Homar leaned over to me. "They got the dark slaves from way to the south, really far down the coast; and the white slaves they got from Gallia I think."

As I watched this perverse game of death play out, I cringed and felt for both sides. I knew none of these men wanted to die or even fight at all, but they had been captured and forced into this profession.

"Terrible, isn't it?" I whispered.

"Queen Madiré has an appetite for terrible things," Homar replied. "And most people in this city don't have a heart for humanity."

The depravity went only worsened in the Arena and I witnessed bloody spectacle after bloody spectacle. Human and elven gladiators, always naked—perhaps due to Madiré's sensual appetites—fought beast after beast. The menagerie was quite remarkable and exotic, full of animals that certainly didn't belong in such a cold climate. There were striped orange jungle cats; great behemoths which Homar called elephants; hordes of rabid lynxes. Plenty of sentient blood was shed, as well, including a game where a lone armed gladiator cut down fifty unarmed and naked criminals.

By the time the games were finished, the dirt floor of the Arena was moist and red with blood. I felt filthy for having watched.

Homar and I ate a dish of cooked snails—a Lonen specialty—at a small tavern nearby the Waning Crescent. We didn't want to eat at the same inn where we earned our coin.

"Madiré certainly takes a liking to bloodshed," I said.

Homar smiled. "I'm not sure what's worst; our druen 'problem,' or hers," he said, placing a snail dripping with oil in his mouth and then biting down. "Rumors say she has an insatiable appetite for the sensual, as well."

"I suppose I don't find that very hard to believe," I said. "After all, most of her gladiators were dressed in nothing."

Homar's voice lowered to a whisper. "Personally, I believe she is mad," he said softly, "and she is very cruel to those who say anything bad about her—she's got spies looking around the city for dissidents. You've witnessed a typical day of entertainment for

Naremon, I'm afraid. There are games every Saturday and they're finding it hard to find enough criminals to kill. Now they're putting people in the Arena for things as simple as missing a tax payment, or stealing bread. All for the queen's entertainment."

"Well I certainly won't do anything wrong, then," I said. "Lest I become cat fodder."

Homar smiled. "As long as you are very careful, I do believe you will be all right. Say nothing bad about the queen, steal nothing from the shopkeepers—basically, be a productive citizen and do nothing wrong."

I bit into the chewy meat and swilled the cooked snail down with some of the cheap white wine that had come with our dinner.

"It has a been a good day, has it not?" he said. "Eventually you will find Naremon to be tolerable, as I have. There are a lot of things to do in this city; you just have to find your crowd."

"I think I have," I said.

That year, Emperor Danthesti of Lamdar crossed over into the disputed province of Zandor. Zandor was rich in goldmines, as it bordered the eastern half of the Dragonteeth Mountains. Danthesti argued that it belonged to him because centuries ago it had belonged to his ancestor. But we Lonen knew very well that the province had been given to us lawfully.

Work at the Waning Crescent Inn was light over the next decade. During those years, a priest from the Upper City named Amon gathered an army of mercenaries and crossed the River Galios southward. He then marched into Kardir to conquer the Plains Elves. Although I admired his ambition, I never thought it was a good thing to conquer a sovereign land.

I grew from youth into young adulthood in Naremon. Although I was tolerated I was not satisfied living here. I never did forget Katrina. Thoughts of her gave me empathy for the human slaves. I did not look on them as inferior, but as real people, and Homar often teased me because of it. But I thought of them as the equal of elves, and I wasn't sure why.

Over the years, my friendship with Homar grew strong and I considered him a brother. Throughout all the bad times and the good times, we stuck together, and when things happened we kept nothing from each other.

In winter of 1103, around my fortieth birthday, the war with the Lamen Elves was proclaimed over. The armies of the Lamen king had claimed a crippling victory at the Battle of Shiron. Some blamed the lost war for Queen Madiré's plummeting spiral into total madness.

Executions were ordered of people she thought were plotting against her. A total of four assassination attempts were "foiled" during that year—none of which were substantiated with evidence—and each "conspirator" was fed to tigers at the Arena. I became especially guarded, saying nothing but good of Madiré except to Homar, late at night, for her spies were everywhere.

CHAPTER NINE: INTO THE PALACE

One morning during late autumn of 1104, Homar and I were delivering a breakfast of eel to an elderly man who lived in our neighborhood. I was shivering, despite being bundled up in heavy layers of clothing.

The Waning Crescent offered delivery services, and as the youngest and fittest druen there, Sildé sent Homar and me to perform the task. The man in question, one Eli of Linen Street, was sick and bedridden and unable to walk to the inn for his meals. Nor was he able to cook for himself. He paid us to feed him.

We had just about turned down the road when a man wearing government regalia approached us. My heart froze in fear. Had Madiré fabricated some tale to justify using us in the gladiatorial games? I thought of running, but then I knew that would make things worse. I doubted I'd be able to escape.

As he got closer, I saw Homar was nearly immobile with fear.

"Hello, gentlemen," he said. "Her Majesty requests your presence at the palace. May I lead you to her?"

"Why?" I said, hoping I didn't look as afraid as I really was. Showing weakness was never an asset in Naremon.

"Do not worry; she has nothing against either of you," the man said. "Now please, come with me."

"We have to deliver some food—" I began but my voice trailed off.

"I'm sure the queen's request is more important than your delivery," the government agent said succinctly. He snatched the eel dish away from my hand, dropped it on the ground, and stomped it to oblivion. Then he bowed. "Now, again, please follow me. The queen wishes to see you."

I eyed Homar nervously, and walked in step with the elven man.

We ascended the Marble Stair to the Upper City and approached the palace grounds. We pushed open the great double doors.

Madiré's palace was beautiful, with great white columns trimmed in gold and indoor gardens; colorfully-painted statues of elven queens past and exquisite paintings that might go for a hundred Yan.

We climbed a bright marble winding staircase, until we entered a spacious wood-paneled hall. Walking down room by room, we eventually came to a large oak door. The government agent knocked, and a frighteningly familiar voice called out, "Come in!"

The queen's room was immense, bigger than the entire Waning Crescent, and huge glass windows, draped with silken purple curtains, looked out into the sprawling villas and mansions of the Upper City. The wooden floor was both varnished and layered in beeswax; and paintings of Londor's countryside hung on the room's white walls. Every piece of furniture—every chair, table and couch—was made with only the best materials and kept impeccably clean. The wall had been painted with bright white-and-red patterns.

I found myself unable to move as the queen entered. She was wearing a red, velvet dress tailored to display her every curve and good feature, and hide her every flaw. She was wearing her thick black hair long and disheveled.

"Ah," she said, smiling coldly. "You have done well, Hanthori. Quite exceptionally well. Now you may leave me while I discuss business with them."

The agent bowed and left, shutting the door quietly as he made his exit.

"Now," Madiré said. "On the bottom level of the palace, towards the back, is a large room dedicated to my entertainment. Have you noticed it there, gentlemen?"

Both Homar and I shook our heads. I looked at Homar, who had grown very pale.

"Hanthori has been scouting out Naremon for the city's finest young men. If you will serve in my 'entertainment room,' I will pay you two hundred Yan a year; if you refuse, I'm not really sure what I'll do with you, but it shan't be pleasant."

I knew what she was insinuating. But angering Madiré was not in my best interests. I said, "Of course."

Homar nodded enthusiastically with a fake smile.

"Good," she said. "Now my handmaiden Silvé will lead you to your proper place."

A young girl wearing a hooded yellow robe came out of the same door Madiré had. She bowed and gestured us to follow her.

There was nothing I wanted less than serving Madiré in this way. Though the grief for Katrina had lost its pointed edge, I sometimes thought she was present and watching over me. I had promised her, "I will not love another."

Silvé led us downstairs to the lower part of the palace and walked through several winding corridors. We came to a red-painted door that read in Elvish "Enter and Enjoy." A man collected tolls there, but Silvé explained that we were new employees and he let us pass.

The doors swung wide, and inside the chamber I witnessed firsthand the depravity of the queen. There were fifteen men inside, both elven and human, and ten women. Each person, male and female, was barely dressed, wearing underwear or nothing at all, reclining on long couches and velvet-lined benches. A nobleman dressed in purple silk and a female prostitute were chatting in one commoner.

A lute player, a flutist, and a drummer played pounding music on a stage in the back of the room, as a naked woman whipped her body sultrily to the beat. The sight made me nauseous.

Silvé quietly ordered us to undress and take our places within the room, then left back through the way she had come. I believe the brothel made Silvé—an innocent girl—very uncomfortable. But she had to do whatever her mistress bade, lest she be marked for death like so many others had been before her.

Over the year, Madiré favored Homar and me greatly, to the point where she lavished her desires on us almost exclusively. During winter of 1104, a deadly plague known as the Demon's Itch spread wide through the brothel, which Madiré caught, and in a fit of anger she ordered everyone to be thrown in jail. After making an indulgent scene of self-pity, weeping and tearing her garments, a few who hadn't developed the foul disease—Homar and I among them—were released a few days later and put back to work in the brothel. Then, on New Year's Day, I was given two hundred golden Yan as promised, enough to buy me a mansion if I wanted one.

Sometime in late spring, I recall, Madiré began calling us King Nocturne and King Homar though she did not have a husband, and told us to stay in the room of a dead prince. The queen furnished it excessively and demanded that the palace servants bring us whatever we needed whenever we asked, that if we were unhappy for a moment she would throw them off Dead Kings' Bluff.

Spring turned to summer and my work in the brothel did not cease. Madiré descended even further into madness, executing people left and right for assassination plots that existed only in her mind, and putting priests whom she disliked into the Arena to die. Sometimes I was forced to go to the Arena and accompany Madiré, watching the spectacle as the King-Consort. I began to plot my escape, but I knew that I was already in deep, that she would try to kill me if I ran away.

Homar and I dared not speak ill of Madiré to each other, even when alone, for she had spies everywhere. I honestly had no idea what she was going to do next. Any supposed sign of "infidelity" toward her was paid back with cruelty.

Madiré demanded I tell her I love her, and if I neglected to do this multiple times each day she would scream and lock herself in her room, making loud weeping noises that I knew were manufactured and insincere. As the days went on, I looked for ways to escape, but no opportunity ever presented itself.

CHAPTER TEN: MADIRÉ Y DRAZZANDORI

The gentle summer heat abated and gave way to autumn. It was the year 1105 and I, as had become the unfortunate pattern, was in bed with Madiré. Outside, through the glass window, I could see snowflakes gracefully falling from the icy gray sky. A great fire was burning in the hearth by the bed, warming our frigid bodies. She had ordered her servants to keep it burning all night, on pain of death. Then, as she lay there playing with my hair, she spoke, and said something that startled me greatly.

"My Head Wizard, Marnisi, says that you are a druen."

"No I'm not," I said, trying my best to hide my surprise, "That's not true. What makes her think that?"

"She discerned it by divination," she said, "She observed the intestines of a slain dove, one of the many methods in which she determines the future. She is a great prophetess as well as a magician. She is my very best... that is why I appointed Marnisi the Head Wizard."

"Oh, that's bogus," I said, "Do you really believe her?"

She grabbed my shoulders and wrenched herself on top of me, looking into my eyes like a tigress ready to devour her prey. "Damn you, Nocturne—show me those long white fangs. Show them to me or else I'll have you hanged."

"I have no fangs!" I said sternly.

Despite my struggle she was strong and managed to pry open my mouth with her long, red-painted fingernails. "I see them!" she cried, eyes glinting with delight as her nails dug into my gums. "Oh, Nocturne; sweet Nocturne, you can drink my blood," she

moaned, "I want you to so badly. No… I don't want it, Nocturne…
I need it. I need you. It's the only thing that will give me pleasure,
honey. Oh, Noct—"

"Stop it!" I hissed and threw her off me, one of the boldest
moves I had ever made in her presence. If done by a man she was
less attached to, it would surely mean his death. "You do *not* want
me to. It's dangerous," I said. But I didn't really care whether it was
dangerous for her. I refused because I still firmly believed in the
Path. I was still Nocturne Dandrinnassi and I did not want to break
the law. "Besides," I said, "I am sworn not to."

"How dare you be sworn to anything but our love!" Madiré
bellowed. She leapt upon me and slapped me hard across the face.
She pressed her naked breasts hard against my chest but they only
sickened me.

I struggled to throw her off me but I couldn't. She grabbed
my shoulders and rolled over so that I was on top of her, and
growled with wild eyes. "Now do it, or I will order you to be burnt
at the stake."

"No!" I roared.

"Damn you, Nocturne!" Madiré screamed, "I am Queen of
Naremon! I have total power over you, and all my citizens! When it
is night I can declare it day and everyone will arise! When it is day I
can declare it night and everyone will go to sleep! I reign supreme.
I am a goddess!"

Enraged, I sunk my teeth deep into her neck and drank
from her veins only a few seconds, feeling a brief euphoria but
quickly pulling out to avoid damage to her body. Blood ran down
my mouth and I smacked my lips to clean myself. "There," I
snarled, "Happy?"

"Oh…" she groaned, "Yes." She did not bleed; with the
bite of a druen came some kind of healing salve, so that when we
removed our fangs, there was no further bleeding. "Will I become

a druen now?"

"No," I said. "That's just a rumor. One cannot become a druen."

"Ah well," said Madiré. She rolled over, throwing me on my side and almost off the bed. She rubbed her arms and legs against the sheets of the bed in ecstasy. "I have become one with my great-grandmother! I have become Dorumé the First, Dorumé the Ultimate."

"What do you mean by that?" I asked.

"Come," she said, "The Court Players will explain it to you with their theatrical performance of *Dorumé y Drazzandori*."

The title of the play was Elvish for "Dorumé and the Druen King" and I had a suspicion of what the play's subject would be. Spending any unnecessary time with Madiré was never a pleasant thought.

The Royal Theater was in the middle story of the palace and could probably seat over a thousand spectators. The theater itself had a lush red carpet, towering marble columns, and a sparkling glass chandelier hanging over the audience. Each chair was lined with red silk—a testament to the decadence of Naremon's elite, the only ones allowed to enter. I had heard the acoustics in the Royal Theater were also nearly perfect, and many musicians performed here.

Being the only spectators, and Madiré and I took a seat at the very front. We waited perhaps ten minutes and the play hadn't started; I thought this typical, but Madiré had begun to stir in her seat and curse. Soon after she had started yelling and making a great fuss, a theater attendant rushed backstage to hurry along the preparations. I heard some arguing from the actors backstage, but then, just moments later, the curtains opened.

A wooden backdrop of the city was revealed. The design and paint made the faux architecture resembled that of Naremon. Standing center stage, in front of the fake city, was a Lonen actress. She wore a fake crown and long, tattered black robes. As she spoke she made broad, emphatic gestures.

"I am Dorumé the Great, queen over the most magnificent city in all the world!" she said, her powerful voice resounding perfectly throughout the theater. "I, Dorumé, formed the first School for Magic in the town of Sirriom. I established the order of Court Wizards. I lifted the prudish ban on Forbidden Magic. I turned Naremon from a frontier town into the greatest city the waking world has ever known. And yet I, the greatest woman in the world of the living, I have not found my love… I have not found a husband. Because there is not a single man in Naremon worthy of me. But perhaps somewhere else, there is."

After the monologue continued for a few minutes, a handmaiden dressed in yellow arrived with a parchment letter in hand. "Madame," she said, her voice equally resonant, "The druen king, Drathanyi, has sent this from his kingdom. Shall I read it to you, Your Majesty?"

"Yes," said Dorumé.

"'Word of your beauty has reached my ears in the far-off frozen wastes of the druen. I wish to visit Naremon and observe the magnificent culture that I have heard very much of, but never experienced firsthand. And I would also like to meet the one who built it.' It is signed: Drathanyi, Lord of the North."

The actress playing Dorumé consented, and after a few more lines, they left the stage and the curtains closed. A few minutes later, they reopened to reveal the arrival of the man in question. The actor who played Drathanyi was a tall, lanky actor wearing a pair of fangs that served to caricature my race. But I said nothing and waited for the play to end.

The remaining hour and a half of the play told of the romance between Queen Dorumé the First and King Drathanyi; their son, Seliri and their daughter, Zané.

But the story ended tragically, when Drathanyi was slain by the Lamen witch-hunter Thorendi. Thorendi was played by an actress who wore horns to indicate his wickedness. One day, while King Drathanyi was hunting, he succeeded in getting past his guards and placing a dagger through his neck.

When news reached Dorumé's ears, she slit her wrists and died. The curtain closed, and the play was over.

Madiré was in tears. I, however, found myself only irritated.

With loving a druen justified in her eyes, I began sleeping in Madiré's private chamber almost every night. I cursed my luck. Each night the pleasure of lying in her bed grew shallower, each night she grew more monstrous to my eyes. I remembered Katrina. What better woman could be found in all Varda, and whom of the greatest daughters of elvenkind could match her?

One night, in an effort to relieve myself from her constant pressure, I informed her that Homar, also, was a druen. Her response was euphoria. The first night, Homar screamed at me for telling her. But I could uphold this burden no longer.

One evening Madiré took me to the Tower of the Wizards to read my fortune. It was there that I saw a hideous woman, fat and covered in boils, flipping through a thick book. Beside her were several other equally fat women. They wore tattered black dresses and silver crescent-moon necklaces.

"Hello, Marnisi," Madiré told the woman.

"Hello," she said in a raspy voice reminded me of a frog.

"What is this man doing in my tower? Only women are allowed to be wizards, you know." She glared.

"I wanted to introduce you to King Nocturne," Madiré said.

"King?" the fat woman growled. "You got rid of King Hadon long ago."

"And Nocturne is my new husband. The new king," Madiré replied. "Now tell me, what spell are you researching, dearest Marnisi?"

"A prosperity spell, to cast over the entire kingdom," she croaked, "It will take the entire court to cast it successfully," Marnisi said, occasionally stopping to give me dirty looks. "Speaking of research... we need more funds to develop alchemy. The Royal Alchemists' Society is the laughing stock of all the nations."

Madiré's tone suddenly sharpened. "You will send a formal request next time, and not snap at me like that. It would bode well for your safety to be more polite, Marnisi."

Together we turned and left. Apparently not all Madiré's friends enjoyed my presence.

Madiré began alternating between Homar and me, saying that we were both Drathanyi embodied, but in different ways. She tried to explain her ridiculous theory by stating Homar was the beautiful body of Drathanyi, while I was his beautiful mind. And that joined together, we had become the embodiment of the ancient romance of her great-grandmother.

Feigning love has never been easy for me, but I tried as best as I could to pretend that I loved Madiré. As I saw her cruelty and madness firsthand, she steadily grew more and more unattractive until she became almost some kind of monster, more a thing than a sentient being.

One night, when Madiré was gone, the handmaiden Silvé appeared in the bedchamber. The yellow-robed girl looked very scared and uncomfortable. She removed her hood and snuck up to me. "Nocturne!" she whispered, her voice shaking. "I've come to tell you of a plot. I overheard the Head Wizard Marnisi talking to Madiré. She prophesied that if Madiré does not kill you and Homar, she will die by the end of the week."

I sat up, eyes wide. "Has she bought into it?"

"Yes!" Silvé whispered, "She plans to poison both you and Homar tomorrow morning at breakfast!"

"Thanks!" I said, "Now get out before you're caught."

She ran away through the door. After a second the panic of the situation hit me. I resolved to go inform Homar. We needed to escape as fast as we could—tonight, preferably, if possible. The thought of losing Homar to this murderess sickened me.

I rushed out the bedroom door and into the hallway. Homar was sleeping in what by now I considered to be "my room"—since it had been my turn to sleep with the monster.

I was stopped by a cold voice, a voice I knew so well.

"Where are you going?" Madiré said from the opposite end of the hall.

I froze and turned around slowly, repressing a glare. Surely enough, there was Madiré, and beside her was the repulsive Marnisi, looking ugly as ever. She was fat like a plump duck, and boils and birthmarks deformed her already-hideous face. Her ugliness took my breath away and I tried not to look at her. In her warped hands she held a crooked wooden staff. She wore a necklace of bone, and a bracelet of bright beads.

"He thinks I am ugly," Marnisi croaked.

"Oh, no he doesn't, he thinks you're beautiful. Everyone does. Don't you, Drathanyi?"

"Of course." I wondered whether the shaky tone of my

voice aroused their suspicion. But I forced my mind to think in the present, to act in the manner that our casual conversation demanded. "Why would I think she is ugly?"

"Many do," Marnisi said, "I have not married before. Does that surprise you, Nocturne?"

"Not at all."

"Oh, enough with the silly games," Madiré laughed. "Go to bed, Marnisi, and keep researching that prosperity spell. I should want a great harvest this year."

"I will research it diligently, love," Marnisi said. Glaring, she departed.

"Now shall we go to bed, Drathanyi?" she said, "Let us make love. Let us make such fiery love, as if it were our last opportunity to do so. Make me happy, Drathanyi! Make me proud to be the wife of the Drazzandori."

"I'll try," I said.

We did make love continuously that night, and we both consumed aphrodisiac after aphrodisiac—*honri* petals, and love potions the Court Wizards had brewed.

In the middle of the night, though, when I ached and my muscles were sore and I was covered in sweat, I suddenly collapsed in fatigue.

I had a horrid dream that night, that Madiré had turned into a bloated demon about to devour me whole. And when I awoke early in the morning, I realized it was not far from the truth.

She was bending over me with a smile. "Arise, sleeper," she said, "Come on, you and Homar are going to treat me to breakfast and make me feel like the goddess that I am." She ran a hand through her black hair. She had already donned her extravagant red dress and doused herself in the specialty perfume which by now smelled like death to me. I would have to stop Homar from eating or drinking at all costs.

For breakfast Madiré had prepared a bowl of fried clams—one for each of us—and a glass of red wine. I eyed the wine, having no doubt that it was the poison agent. She herself had a glass as well, which was doubtlessly free of her tampering.

"So, Drathanyi the Body and Drathanyi the Mind are joined together at my table over breakfast," Madiré said, "And I have become convinced that our spirits are one, even after death."

"Do you think we are going to die soon?" I said.

She looked at me with what I knew was surprise, but recovered with grace. "Why, no," she said. "Of course not. Now enjoy your clams, and drink your wine. We got it from human vineyards; it should be a nice break from the Arlomhic vintage we usually have."

Homar put the wineglass to his lips.

"Don't drink it!" I yelled and swept my hand towards the glass. But I missed, and Homar had already drunken deeply of the cup.

I stood up, shaking, blood boiling, no longer caring about my safety. I let out all the energy pent up over the months, the years, I had served Madiré. I overturned the table. The bottle of wine smashed into a thousand shards. The bowls and the plates fell with a splintering crash. Madiré stood up, her eyes burning.

But I hated her even more than she hated me. "Damn you, Madiré!" I screamed. "You monster!"

I leapt to my feet and punched her against the jaw as hard as my arm could swing. She fell back, unconscious.

Meanwhile, Homar's face turned white, losing what little color it had had before. He grasped at his throat, gulped for air, and fell back in his chair.

"I hate you, Madiré! I do not love you! I never loved you!" I screamed.

I did not kill her, though I could have, and by my blood I wanted to; but there was too little time and I didn't want to complicate things. More than revenge, I wanted escape.

I tore off my shirt and donned a green tunic. Then, knowing that once I had gone I would need money, I headed to the sack where I had stored all the Yan I had earned from serving the monster.

Into my knapsack I poured as many of the gold coins that could fit, then threw it over my shoulders and walked off to make a slow, casual exit.

I acted as typically as I could and moved through the palace. I headed down the stairs without a single glance behind me. The royal servants were still at work, shining the silvers or sweeping or waxing the floors. They paid me no heed. In fact they tried not to look at King Nocturne, lest they incur his wrath.

I made it out of the palace itself and into the courtyard. No one had seemed to notice my leaving, but that did not last long.

By the time I had made it down the Marble Stair and escaped into the Lower City, the skeleton guards had somehow been informed of my escape, perhaps by the wizards who controlled them. Perhaps Marnisi had come to see whether her plans had been finalized, and then found her love stricken nearly dead on the floor.

As I crossed down the main road, a group of the skeletons began pursuing me. I sprinted as fast as I could, pushing pedestrians aside. Soon the whole city guard was after me, but skeletons do not make fast runners, and very few elves served as guards.

I dashed quickly out of the west gate and dove into the shade of a nearby forest. I waited there until night, hiding in the thick underbrush, and when I was certain that they had given up on the search, I stirred from my hiding place and made toward the countryside, toward freedom.

CHAPTER ELEVEN: BJORN

I was forty-four. I was free. I had escaped Madiré.

Feeling confident and unchallenged, I took a year to wander aimlessly through the Elf Lands, through the life that had never been available to me as a druen. I no longer worked at the Waning Crescent; and although I was also free from the restrictions Sildé had placed on me, I tried my best to follow the Path of Dandrinnas. I still believed it was the best way a druen should live; it was the only way to overcome Gilden's Curse.

I made sure my fangs were retracted at all times; I never looked hungrily upon a potential victim and therefore never got aroused. The blood of sentient man would never enter me, I swore.

When I crossed from the dark forests of Londor into the vast kingdom of the Lamen Elves, I followed their customs as best I could. I dressed like the natives in bright golds and yellows, and donned flame orange robes during temple services. The fifty or so Yan I managed to salvage were more than enough to pay for anything I could ever desire.

The kingdom of the Lamen grew incredibly tame as I progressed further west—an land of endless wheat fields and bean fields and vineyards and apple orchards. Few wild trees grew there. Farms and cities dominated nearly every mile, and I had never seen a country so thoroughly cultivated in my life. After a while it depressed me not to see things that the plow hadn't yet touched— the vast pine taiga of Drastheon and the open sea filled with fish. Even Londor, with its sizeable cities, was wilder than this. Perhaps I liked nature better than I thought.

It was late autumn. The wheat had been cut long ago, and the grapes had recently been picked from the vine. And it was now that I found myself racing down a country road on the white stallion that I had bought, not really sure where I was going, planning to stop at the next village and relax at the local inn. My coinpurse was not going to be empty for a very long time.

Eventually I ascended a great hill and saw in the distance the shores of a cold gray sea, surrounded by pines. The waves waxed huge before crashing onto the sandy shore. I realized I had come to the Western Sea after months of wandering. I had heard that this sea exists, but never once in my childhood had I thought I would ever see it.

I approached, galloping down the hill, and got to the water's edge in a few minutes' time. As I did the heavens opened and a fresh rain began pouring—icy rain that made me want to get indoors as fast as I could, but I didn't. The cold water trickled down my cheek and dampened my tunic, the coarse silvery sand of the shore soon darkened. I could see several crabs crawling along. They would make a good dinner, if necessary.

Across the elven Sea to the west was the land of the Umen—or the Forest Elves as they were informally known—the best archers in all the Elf Lands; friends of beasts, deer whisperers and barbarians. I could not see far beyond the stormy waters, but I knew that noble yet savage land was very near.

Thunder rolled across the hills; I opened my mouth, and rain dribbled in. I was free.

But I found that the Elf Lands bored me; I felt too much a part of them. I still had not forgotten about Katrina, the human girl sweeter than any elf I had ever known. I had grown tired of my own kind.

That evening I pulled my steed southward along the shore, towards the mountains, and started off quickly down the path I had chosen.

I did not lie to myself; I knew very well where I was going. Southward into kingdoms of humanity.

Great steely mountains appeared in the horizon—giant mounds of stone capped with snow. They were the Dragonteeth, and I knew I was getting close. As the rain gushed and the sky darkened, the farmland diminished. I drew near a forest of pines. The land grew wild and I found myself in the quiet peace of the wilderness.

The air was a bit warmer near the shore. But the land was cold, even uncomfortably so in the scant furs I had brought. The coast, however, was more temperate than the mainland and snow fell only rarely.

I rode for three days through the coastal rainforest, dining on rabbit, clam, crab, or fish. I found food both in the sea and in the woods, and I generally ate the meat uncooked. Berries were quite plentiful here, and although they didn't make for a filling meal they made great treats.

On the morning of the fourth day the weather had calmed down, and a bit of sunlight glanced through the clouds. It had rained almost nonstop through my travels along the coast. As I groggily awoke I found that my horse had run off and escaped; I had thought her more loyal than she actually was. So I set off on foot.

I traveled down the beach, keeping an eye on the woods with *Dreské* and *Dreské* close at hand. I soon arrived at a boat beached on the shore.

A sleek and graceful ship—perhaps seventy feet in length—it boasted thirty pairs of oars and a wide square sail. Embroidered on the sail was the stylized image of a green dragon.

The head of a grotesque monster had been carved on the prow. Elves had not built this ship.

I took one step closer to observe it further, when I heard the underbrush crackling behind me. I whipped around and drew *Dreské* ringing from its sheath.

Out of the forest's cool gloom a human man emerged. He was tall, perhaps six feet, and lanky. His skin was rosy, not the corpselike hue of mine, and he had a thick blonde beard. In his right hand he gripped a heavy steel axe; in his left, a wooden shield.

"Aye!" he bellowed, staring at me with his fiery blue eyes, "An elf, 'ave we? Spare any coin for my king, Ragnar? Or will I have to bleed it out of ye?"

I pointed my daggers toward him and took a cautious step back, giving him a very stern look. "I would not be so greedy if I were you," I said, "I've killed hundreds—no, thousands—of men like yourself."

"And I have braved the North Seas, and the South Seas, and the stormy ocean, and sailed to the frozen wastes and the seething jungles in search of gold. I doubt you have killed as many as I."

For the first time in years I willingly extended my fangs. The warrior stepped back, frightened just a bit.

"What is your name, little man?" I hissed.

Raising his axe high over his head, he thundered back an answer without the slightest trace of fear in his voice. "I am Bjorn son of Advard, husband to Beona and great-grandson of Helgur himself. I do not fear thee, monster! Not one lick!"

I could not help but admire his bravery. I took one step backwards and forced my fangs to retract. I softened my gaze. "I do not want to harm you, Bjorn," I said, "I came to the human lands with nothing but the best wishes to your race, mankind."

"I was kept here to watch the boat," Bjorn he said, eyes

burning. "The men are out on a raid on some of half-breed village, and will be returning soon. Ye'd better scurry off before I change my mind about letting ye go, you elvish dog!"

I found his change of demeanor remarkable—now, without the threat of danger, he had gone from fearless martyr to mean-hearted scalawag again. But I was not one to be threatened.

"I am *not* a dog," I said, narrowing my eyes. I pitched *Dreské* back and *Dreské* forward, taking what Aldor had called the viper stance. "If there is any dog here, it is you, Bjorn Advardsson."

He swung his axe hard at me and I swept the blow away with *Dreské*. The steel dagger bit into the axe's wooden haft. Once again I let my fangs show and hissed.

He swept the axe at me again; I blocked easily. A few blows later, I dropped the daggers and leapt upon him with all fours. I had told myself I would not break the Oath of Dandrinnas—not ever. But then I began to question the Oath on impulse, as I saw his pink, pink neck and the blood that so freely flowed through his veins.

A loud voice echoed through the woods.

"Get off Bjorn, ye long-toothed monster!" a voice thundered from behind. In the blink of an eye I broke his grip and leapt back a few feet near a tree to face my aggressor.

He was a middle-aged man with flame-red hair and many scars. He was pot-bellied and in his coarse, gruff hands he held an enormous double-bitted axe. Thirty other men—each tall and bright-haired like their brethren—stood behind carrying sacks of silver and gold coins and steel weaponry that clearly wasn't theirs.

"Who are ye, monster?"

"Nocturne," I said. "Dralynthi, in my own tongue. Son of Drethori and Drassané." I knew that they would have no idea where Nardur was, that it was the land of vampires hated and feared by all elves. I doubted they knew much about elvenkind at all.

"Leave us be, monster," the red-bearded man said.

"A'right? We just want to be left alone. We go back home, you don't cause any trouble—that's our deal."

"I don't mean to harm you," I said. "What's your name?"

He gave me a wayward glance. Eventually he said, "Ragnar—King Ragnar. Son of Ragni. I hail from Badelgard. You know where that is, monster?"

I shook my head.

"It's south o' where you're standin'. We live in Skarn Harbor."

"Can I come with you?"

"Ha!" Ragnar said. "We don't normally be allowin' monsters to live in Skarn."

"I could be of great assistance to you," I said. "I'm a good warrior—I could help you raid. You could be one man stronger.

Ragnar raised a brow. "Well…" He eyed his comrades. "Ye downed Bjorn, and he's the finest fighter we've got. I s'pose you can join us, 'long as you don't pull any monstrous moves on us, eh? Tonight we sail home for Skarn Harbor and dine in my hall. All right? We've got some beautiful women—but don't you touch any of 'em. We don't want to pollute our human blood with elves."

I smiled. A human woman was the finest breed of woman and I hadn't enjoyed the company of one since Katrina. Either way, some rest and relaxation was well-needed.

"Great," I finally answered, "I will join you, Ragnar son of Ragni." I grabbed as Bjorn gave me an unsure glance. Perhaps he hadn't yet forgiven me for frightening him. I hoped to apologize to him later.

I headed toward the boat as the Badelgarders prepared to set off.

After we got into deeper waters we hoisted up the sail and

hugged the shore for about two hours, sailing alongside the gorgeous rocky fjords. The landscape of Badelgard was rocky and scenic, a wilderness that I didn't think would be conducive to agriculture. It was a land where things out of dreams—dragons; horn-helmed heroes; icy, blue-haired giant maidens—walked in the full sight of men.

Before long the sailors rolled up the mainsail and pulled out their oars, steering the boat carefully into the mouth of a gushing river as they worked hard against the current. Their sweat-slicked muscles glistened as they heaved and pulled through the swift waters. Meanwhile, King Ragnar stood on the prow, peering into the horizon and barking orders.

The oarsmen sang in chorus as they rowed; it was how they passed the time and got through each heave and pull.

Skruga! Skruga! Green-scaled Skruga!
You are the sound of the pealing horn
You are the taste of mead on the tongue
And the wind of my sail

Some time when darkness had fallen over the land—when I had long fallen asleep on the pinewood bench that I had been given—I awoke to the raiders' shouts as they tied their longboat to the wooden dock. That in itself was not a great feat, but they also had to bring the loot from their last raid ashore. Among the treasures, I saw a few brightly-painted driftwood totems, silver-lined ritual knives and uncut gems.

A short walk inland, I saw a gathering of wooden houses lit with candles and a huge wooden hall on a hill. I heard the dreamy strain of lutes and harps and singing voices resonating from inside the hall.

Before I walked in I saw Bjorn standing alone near the

docks and approached him. "Hey, Bjorn," I said. "I'm sorry for attacking you."

Bjorn grunted.

"Did you hear me? I said I'm—"

"Yeah, I heard ye."

"Well—"

He gripped my shoulder tightly with his hands. "Ye haven't learned your place in Skarn, Alfy. You'd better learn it, quick. I meant the part about elves bein' dogs."

He left me and headed toward the mead hall. For a moment I only stood there, wondering what I had done wrong.

Inside the great hall—the Mead Hall, as they called it—I could see hundreds of wooden kegs crammed wherever space allowed, and four fire pits where whole pigs and lambs were roasting on spits. Surrounding each fireplace were Badelgarders on wooden benches and chairs.

Busty blue-eyed girls wandered the grounds with jugs of mead, wearing tight, short-cut dresses. I took a seat by one of the fire pits and warmed my frigid wet body on the fire. The warmth flooded over me, slowly burning away the chill that had sunk so deep into my body.

I felt someone tap on my shoulder. I quickly turned my head to look.

Standing there was a proud-eyed woman with thick red hair tied into a braid, and sky-blue eyes. She had full red lips and unblemished skin. She had a bit of padding to her but it did not make her unattractive. She, too, was wearing one of those short-cut dresses. Perhaps it was the uniform attire in the Mead Hall.

"Can I get you some mead, good sir?"

"Certainly," I said. "What's your name, lass?"

"I am called Inga," she said.

I smiled warmly.

"I am the daughter of Lafi Greenleaf," she continued, "He was on the raid with you." She bent over closer to me so I could see her breasts. "And you are an elf, I see. What is your name, corpse-skin?"

"Nocturne," I replied.

"What a nice name," Inga whispered. Her breath reeked of alcohol. "Find me later, when the night here is done."

I smiled.

"Now let me get you your mead," Inga said, procuring a giant mug and pouring the contents of her pitcher within. "Enjoy, Alfy." Then she walked off.

The drink tasted like honey on first taste. It was gentle and had dreamlike quality, and I liked it better than all of the finest of the wines I had drunk in Madiré's court.

The starry night deepened as I sipped my dreamy mead, enveloped in its warmth and power. As I downed mug after mug, it began to take effect. I lost all semblance of judgment and laughed at everything.

King Ragnar leapt upon a table and raised his mead mug high, clearly drunk. "This day we slew a whole village o' half breeds. The coast of the Elven Sea is filled with those descendants of humans who bastardized their race with elvish blood! And now I'm feeling a bit tired." He let out a loud burp that lasted perhaps three seconds and then without warning collapsed on the table to the clattering of plates and dishes.

I laughed until I cried. I saw Inga coming toward me. My vision blurred. I have a vague memory of Inga leading me out of the hall and toward her house—and a faint protest to her as she undressed—but I remember nothing more of the night in the mead hall.

CHAPTER TWELVE: THE HUNT

I awoke in bed alone. Outside, a steady rain was pouring from the gray sky and soaking the grass. I heard a rumble of thunder in the distance.

A very sharp pain lingered in my head, my punishment for indulging in good drink last night, but I ignored it and groggily stood up. I was naked. And I wasn't about to go outside without clothes. Grumbling, I pulled on my tunic and leggings that had been discarded by the bed. I stretched and yawned and had a distinct feeling of unease, not for any reason but the pelting rain and thunder.

I walked outside, feeling the droplets hit my face and hair. Lightning flashed in the morning sky. As I walked outside I saw Skarn Harbor looked even more dismal, even tinier in the darkness than it had in the daylight. As for agriculture, a few scattered apple trees and a little apiary for the mead were all the village could boast.

Beyond the tiny village was a deep, dark forest of pines. And far to the north I saw the Dragonteeth Mountains, the purplish behemoths still capped in snow.

"Nocturne!" Inga said behind me. She walked toward me, coming from the Mead Hall. "You are a late riser, sweetheart." She hugged me tightly.

I turned around to look at her. She looked less pretty than she had last night; her hair was wet and disheveled. "Where is everyone?" I said.

"Bjorn and a few of the men are out fishing. King Ragnar is inside the hall still, planning the next raid."

"And where do you think they are going to raid next, Inga?" I asked.

"They've looted the Elf Coast dry, methinks. The treasure there's been picked to death, and needs time to replenish," Inga said, "They might try the Far South, but I doubt it. Come to think of it, they haven't gone after the Zarubes for a while."

"The Zarubes?"

"Zarubain's the land south of the river, darling," Inga said, "They are civilized folk and have a better military than the half breeds. Their knights are the best in the world."

I shivered and wrapped my cloak just a bit tighter around my shoulders. The morning was cold and humid and I could feel the moisture from the rain moving up my legs. I turned toward the hall where a warm fire was probably burning. Inga followed, just a step behind.

Ragnar was arguing back and forth with a few other kings from neighboring villages about which city to raid next. I sat and warmed myself by the fire with Inga as they came to a consensus. Eventually they agreed to raid a city on the western coast of Zarubain called Stormhold, a city of about six thousand. It was small enough to be reasonably undefended, and large enough to be reasonably profitable, but the main attraction was the fact that it completely lacked walls. And cities without walls were a rarity on the Storm Coast, or in Zarubain in general.

The other Badelgardic kings would join together in a massive raiding force that Friday, at the predetermined meeting spot. Shortly after the meeting, the kings departed to carry the news far and wide.

At this point blonde Lafi Greenleaf, Inga's father, approached me. "Hey, Alfy, come with me," he said.

I stood up and followed him outside.

When we were just outside the doors of the mead hall, he threw me against the wall with both his fists. "Damn ye, Nocturne, sleepin' with my daughter! You're an elf, damn you, ye keep to yourself. You hear?"

"I was drunk—I know I shouldn't h—"

"I don't care if you was drunk. You keep your hands off my daughter! You'd better never do that again, or I'll make sure you wish you were dead! I can make your life a living hell, ye know! What if you got her pregnant? Does that sound fun to you? Well it sure as hell don't sound fun to me! I'd lose my reputation! A half breed grandfather."

"Yes! I'm sorry—"

"Sorry ain't good enough, lad! Sorry won't ever be good enough for me!"

"Well it won't happen again!"

"It better not! By Skruga, it better not, or I will come after you! I will kill you, Alfy!" Lafi roared, "D'you hear that? I will kill you if you ever touch my daughter again!" His veins bulged and burned pink as he held me against the wall with his shaking hands. "Ye understand?"

"Yes," I said hoarsely, "I—I'm sorry." I noticed my voice was shaking. I wiped my eyes.

He slapped me on the shoulder. "Glad we had this talk," Lafi said. "Now don't be a cryin' little girl. Ye'd better toughen up if you're going to be raiding with us, a'right?"

I nodded slowly. In the distance I could see Bjorn and the other warriors returning from fishing. As they walked along the river's edge, I noticed their nets were full of trout and herring— some still wriggling and some dead.

The fishermen took their catch inside into the hall, and seared them on the fire until the crispy bodies of the herring seethed with hot juice. I grabbed one, dashed it to taste with salt and pepper and sprinkled on some hot spices the men of Skarn had collected from raids in the Far South.

As I took a bite out of the fish, I heard Inga walking up to me from behind. I turned to look at her; she was smiling at me, completely unaware.

"Hello, Nocturne!" she said cheerfully. "Enjoying your fish, sweetheart?"

"No—Inga—no, we can't—"

She stooped over and planted a wet kiss on my cheek. Instinctively I pushed her away, perhaps with a bit too much force. "What? Why did you do that?" she asked, sounding baffled.

"Your father—he'll kill me if he sees us together. He just threatened to put my head on a pike, Inga. We can't talk to each other anymore—I'm sorry."

Inga stared at me, perplexed, for a few seconds, then sighed. "My dad doesn't have to know. We can keep it a secret, Nocturne." A smile slowly emerged on her lips. "Perhaps it will be more exciting that way!"

I scowled. "Inga, this isn't going to work out. It's just not going to happen."

Her jaw slackened and her eyes turned to a glare. "Don't listen to my father, Nocturne. Are you too much of a coward to go against my father's wishes? He couldn't harm you—he's old, and he's a terrible warrior. Maybe the worst of all the Skarn Harbormen."

"If I *do* go against his wishes, I'll have Ragnar to answer to," I said. "And if Ragnar gets angry, the whole clan will be."

"Don't be a coward, Nocturne. I thought you were much better and braver than this!" Inga said, crossing her arms.

"No." My tone made no room for argument. I turned back to my fish and began nibbling at it absently.

Inga scoffed and struck me on the back with her hand.

"Well then I don't like you, either, Alfy."

Some time shortly after I had finished my fish and licked the salt off my fingers, Ragnar leapt upon the table. He had bits of herring and a few dribbles of mead trapped in his flame orange beard. He beat his chest. "Have you ruffians ever heard of the famed wild boar called Bigbristle?"

"Of course!" a chorus of men called back. I scooted in my seat and listened intensely.

"The Boar from Hell was spotted in Alarrsbork last night! What do you say of getting that beast, an' putting his head on display fer all to see in our hall! All in favor, say I!"

"I!" they all cried in unison.

The hunt was arranged quickly outside the Mead Hall. Only Ragnar and five of the men would go on the hunt, and they were provided with horses. To my surprise, I was one of them.

"This'll make sure the boar doesn't charge you too close!" Ragnar said and handed me a specialized spear with a cross-hilt. I believed that our king had gone on the hunt before, many times; and had downed animals much greater than simple deer. I had the lurking suspicion that there truly were dragons hidden away this mystical, rustic land, though according to scholars they had all died out long ago.

Fifteen bloodhounds were freed from Ragnar's kennels to participate in the hunt, as well. The hounds had been kept fit and always a little underfed to prepare for the hunt. They were not pampered household pets, but vicious and loyal predators.

It was about the third hour that we set out. The bloodhounds ran alongside us and they kept up quite well with horses. I believe they were trained to follow Ragnar's lead.

We made it to Alarrsbork within an hour. The town was tiny, even tinier than Skarn, with only four wooden houses. Apiaries seemed to be its only resource, but the men of Badelgard drank mead heavily, so the beehives probably turned a quite profitable trade.

Guiding his horse with his knees, Ragnar led the hunting party up to the nearest villager—a woman gathering water from the well. "Have you seen Bigbristle?"

"Not since last night!" she said.

We went from person to person in Alarrsbork—knocking on doors and approaching strangers—until at last we uncovered a scrap of information. A woman who hadn't been able sleep claimed to have seen him heading north at midnight through the wilderness, towards a place she called Hrungar Hill.

Ragnar seemed to know exactly where Hrungar Hill was, and without a word he suddenly took off away from the city. We galloped after him and the bloodhounds followed his lead.

We rode quickly through the rocky pine forest. The bloodhounds barked and bayed as they dashed alongside the horses. As we rode, I couldn't help but appreciate the scenic nature of Badelgard. The land itself was rather rocky—an attribute due, I believed, to its nearness to the mountains—but still, Mother Nature gave it plenty of greenery. Patches of scrub pines grew from the rock, and ponds and lakes dotted the area. It was a great spot for hunting, but the soil was not conducive to agriculture, perhaps one of the reasons why Badelgarders had adopted a raiding lifestyle. It was hard to support a burgeoning population when you didn't have access to farms.

I didn't have to ask if we had reached Hrungar Hill; I knew

it when I saw it. The great mound of rock towered before me, making me feel insignificant. The Hill was immense, perhaps two hundred feet in height, and many plants still managed to grow all over it—thorny weeds and awkwardly-rooted pines. At the base of Hrungar Hill sat a pool of water surrounded by trees.

As soon as we arrived the bloodhounds began barking. Sniffing something, they sprinted towards the pool. We kicked our stirrups and pursued the dogs as quickly as we could.

The dogs ran right up to the target, and it was indeed the creature we had been looking for.

Bigbristle was the largest boar I had ever seen in my life. Within seconds of the bloodhounds' attack, he impaled one of the dogs with his tusks, which were probably five feet in length. The monster was four hundred pounds. Against one of us hunters alone, the boar would impale him within seconds.

We circled him, thrusting at Bigbristle with our heavy spears, but his hide was very thick and the spears could not pierce it easily. The bloodhounds were fighting the best they could, but they weren't doing very much damage either. When Bigbristle charged my horse, I bucked away and galloped away a few yards. A thrill surged through my veins like ice. I wheeled back around. This, truly, was what they called the thrill of the hunt.

The more weak wounds we dealt Bigbristle—the more little scrapes and cuts he received from our spears—the wilder he became. His bristles stood on end as he squealed with rage. By the first ten minutes of battle he had already impaled seven of our fifteen bloodhounds, and almost struck a killing blow to one of the huntsmen's horses.

In a stroke of luck, despite the fact that I was no seasoned boar hunter, I delivered a lucky strike to Bigbristle's pelvic area. The skin ruptured and blood started gushing by the bucketful out of the boar's veins. As the pig bucked blindly at his pursuers, losing his orientation and going wild with anger, something deep inside me felt sorry for the dying beast.

Ragnar cheered. "Hooray for Alfy!"

I smiled. The victory was not without cost; I knew I had taken a life. But as the boar squealed and squealed, going mad in his death, there was something that told me perhaps Bigbristle had enjoyed the last hour of his life, that beyond his terror he, also, had enjoyed the thrill of the hunt.

We rode through the forest slowly, dragging the corpse of Bigbristle along from Hrungar Hill to Alarrsbork and then back to Skarn Harbor. The process was tiring, and we did not return until dusk had set over the sky. Ragnar walked by my side and lifted my arm high. He was smiling, and I knew he was very proud that I had struck the killing blow to Bigbristle.

"Alfy killed the boar!" he roared to the Harbormen who were drinking mead inside the Hall. "Li'l Nocturne isn't as useless as we thought! Everyone give a big cheer for Alfy!"

The Harbormen inside the Hall roared, and for once I felt welcome the men of Skarn. We walked together inside, and I saw no one had served dinner yet; they were planning on serving boar.

"Come with me, Nocturne!" Ragnar said, "You will sit by my side at the head of the Hall. You're one of us, now!"

I smiled and followed the King of Skarn Harbor up to the High Table. His table was raised above the rest. I sat down on one of the plush silk cushions that lined the fine oaken chairs. In front of Ragnar's chair, I saw a large bronze saucer with fish bones—the plate he had used for lunch still had not been taken away.

He turned to me and lowered his voice so that only I could

hear. "That doesn't mean you've got full privileges yet," said Ragnar. "You still can't sleep with any of our women, a'right? I heard you slept with poor Inga—that is not acceptable, and won't ever be acceptable, ye hear? We can't be like the half-breeds. The half-breeds are partially related to us—they are humans with roots in Badelgard, but they mixed with the Forest Elves an' now they're a bunch of mutts. You can sit with us, yes; you can eat with us, and hunt with us, and raid with us. But you can't marry any of our daughters. Understand?"

I nodded.

As I watched one of the men of Skarn chop off Bigbristle's head with an axe, I noticed Inga flirting with one of the clansmen. She had forgotten about me quickly.

That evening, we ate a grand feast of pork. And for the next three nights, the corpse of Bigbristle proved enough meat to feed the whole clan.

CHAPTER THIRTEEN: STORMHOLD

In the days after the hunt for Bigbristle, my mind returned once again to the imminent raid, the call for blood. Stormhold awaited our plundering hands.

At a grove just outside Skarn, ten pigs were brought out of their sties and slaughtered one by one on a stone altar to Tyr, the god whom Ragnar held in highest regard. This sacrifice, made a day before the raid, would ensure a swift and overwhelming victory on the side of the Badelgarders.

The boats would set off early in the morning to meet the other clans at their traditional meeting place, Misty Cove, on the rocky southern coast of Badelgard.

Soon, we would steer our boat toward the setting sun and slice boldly through the waves, singing in chorus of blood and strife and victory. Raiding was a way of life for these people, or life itself.

We set off, letting the current take us downriver, out of the mouth and into the open sea. We got a few hundred yards out, then arced sharply left to follow the coast and hoisted the sail.

I tightened my cloak. The sea was a bit choppy that day and occasionally a bit of icy ocean froth would hit my face, reminding me that the North Sea was far too cold for swimming. But the seasoned sailors and explorers of Badelgard were capable and strong-armed and prepared for anything Lorne, god of the sea, could possibly throw their way. I felt safe in their company.

We arrived at Misty Cove on Saturday at noon. It was a

spacious rocky cave off the coast. The walls were covered in graffiti: names of warriors hewn into the rock, runes of good fortune and pictures of the hideous sea monsters they had hewn to the murky depths. Several ships full of Badelgarder raiders had already arrived and beached inside the cove. There were perhaps two hundred of the men gathered by campfires, the metal of their swords and axes and spears glinting in the flickering light.

By noon all ten raiding parties had joined together at Misty Cove and I could hear King Ragnar explaining to his countrymen that I was not an enemy, that I was off limits as a source of plunder.

His friends had gathered from every corner of Badelgard. And though it was a rather small and disorganized nation, a head count proved that the warriors numbered just over four thousand, more than enough to seriously threaten a town like Stormhold.

At about the third hour, a fog crept out of the sea, and I could smell the sweet scent of saltwater and feel its cool embrace. I stepped out of the cove, hopping over rocks as I saw fit, and turned to head a bit further inland.

In a small valley just outside the cove, Ragnar's men ate and replenished their bodies for tomorrow's battle. But no mead was drunk—not a single drop—for tomorrow they had to have their wits about them.

I sat down beside the wonderfully warm fire and rubbed my hands together in the heat.

"Oh, Forni, no one cares about yer silly little adventures!" grumbled Bjorn in his barrel-throated voice, "Did I tell you the time Freidmund and I and a few others sailed my mighty ship, the Sea Spray, into the edge of the world? We sailed 'er about a thousand miles in, an' we got to where no man has been before, I swear it. An' we saw the kraken—big, nasty, tentacled beastie. That sucker's head is the size of an island and it could swallow anything."

"And I suppose you killed it!" said a young, flame-bearded man whom I assumed was Forni.

Bjorn laughed. "No one can kill the kraken. It is Lorne's hound, the sea god's most favored pet, and there is no man strong enough to kill it. Nor any beast. Not even mighty Lord Skruga could kill the kraken."

Forni and a few others stood up with their spears. "How dare you blaspheme Lord Skruga!" Forni roared, "Why, I'll have your head on a pike! I'll give you the Bloody Eagle!"

"I'd like to see you try to put a hand on me!" Bjorn roared and stood up with twice Forni's aggression.

"Settle down!" Ragnar screamed, "Shut your bloody traps! Will I have to banish you children to opposite sides of camp?"

By this time I had surmised that Skruga was some draconic god they worshipped, a great drake who through years of embellishment and idealization had eventually achieved the status of a deity among the men of Badelgard. I doubted the Green Drake's origins were as great as the Badelgarders said, but I dared not say that aloud.

"Now listen up," Ragnar began, "Tomorrow we steer south, before sunrise. Stormhold is around seventy-five miles south of here on the shore, and with luck we should arrive well before nightfall. We surprise them, cut them down, and bring home any golden and silver trinkets you may find. Understood? Take everything of value to me for assessment. All of you will be divied out an equal share, and anyone who steals will have his hands cut off with my sword!"

The Badelgarders nodded, though I doubt they were paying much attention. This was probably routine for them. Out of the corner of my eye I saw that Forni was still giving Bjorn angry looks.

The oarsmen relaxed the next morning and allowed the sail to do most of the work as the fleet steadily drew south. From sunrise until late afternoon we moved swiftly along the waters, just out of sight of the shore, so as not to alert the attention of the Zarube navies that might be patrolling the coast, or the kingdom's many tall watchtowers and lighthouses that kept a keen eye out for ruffians such as we. I knew we were passing by several cities; Zarubad, the capital, being one of them.

We stopped at some point and regrouped, then rolled up the sail and drew our oars. Our fleet of seventy five boats rowed furiously towards the shore, and soon I got my first glimpse of the city of Stormhold.

It was neither a metropolis nor a village, but something in between. By the shore was an extensive network of docks, and a cluster of city shops and houses. I could see several trading ships docked in the harbor, and a great castle that overlooked the whole place on a hill.

Like Ragnar had mentioned, it had no defensive walls, although it looked like they had begun the construction of some on the outskirts.

The sun was just beginning to set when the raid truly began. Badelgardic battle tactics included using shock to their fullest potential. They made sure their reputation as merciless pillagers never faded, that they were never seen as forgiving to those who resisted them. But they also made sure their victims knew that they would not harm those who did not resist. To those who did not fight to save their possessions or village, they showed a sick kind of mercy.

Immediately we set upon the unsuspecting citizens of Stormhold, yelling and making noise, screaming about setting the town aflame for the glory of the Green Dragon, Skruga, and killing every man who dared resist. The lord of the city fled for the castle and narrowly evaded our spears, successfully getting inside before it was too late. He barricaded himself in the keep while a force of about a thousand unskilled militiamen and a hundred or so men-at-arms resisted the Badelgarder raiders.

I fought them with my daggers *Dreské* and *Dreské*, tempted to drink their blood but determined to resist for the glory of Dandrinnas. I did not strike down any woman or child; in fact, I avoided bloodshed as best I could. I felt a bit guilty fighting on the side of these raiders, but I wanted to become their brother; I wanted, beyond anything else, to be human.

The battle lasted well into the late hours of the night, and during the process I was forced into killing two men-at-arms who were attacking me. The Badelgarders, however, showed no such restraint; their mind was filled with lust for gold and silver and jewels. The lives of the men and women of Stormhold were secondary.

Throughout the day I received a few blows to my body, including a deep slash across my arm which had to be dressed with bandages, and a hard blow of the cudgel which broke a few ribs.

We were sure the lord of the city had called for the assistance of all the outlying country barons. The distant country manors had a greater supply of well-armed knights and well-trained men at arms, and they would arrive in hours. So Ragnar and the other Badelgardic kings shouted orders at the men, and made sure that the plundering was conducted with organization and swiftness.

By sunrise all the resistance was crushed, and we ran freely through the city to collect our loot. From the temple of a goddess named Genevieve I collected a jeweled golden chalice and a silver candelabra, shoving it in the bag Ragnar had given me. From the temple of a goddess called Feanara I collected several ceremonial swords, a golden offering plate, and the silver shell of a reliquary. From various homes I found little bits of silver, and by the time the sun rose I was a rich druen.

I gave my share to King Ragnar, who was storing all his men's loot under the trapdoor of a large-hulled ship.

The warriors carried off everything of value they could find. They searched home after home for every spare coin, then burnt down the residences when they were done.

There were many deaths that day that should never have occurred. Many panicked, innocent villagers were struck dead in the Stormhold streets; and for the most part, the Badelgarders had no sympathy for the murdered. But I like to believe they had no choice; they had been brought up to think like raiders, and they had no other way to survive. Still, I could see why other peoples saw them as heartless monsters.

The burning thatch of Stormhold caused a great cloud of smoke to arise, and we knew this would quickly draw outside help. The night deepened, and the darkness hung heavy o'er our hearts, and by the time sunrise came we were still not finished depriving the town of its loot.

The lord of Stormhold and some villagers endured the siege by holing up within the fortified castle walls. Ragnar and a troupe of warriors stood outside and heckled them, using every insult he knew. But no matter how many times Ragnar accused him of cowardice, the lord of Stormhold would not stir from his shelter.

Soon our concerns were confirmed; he had sent for help abroad. Just after sunrise, one of the Badelgardic sentries reported Zarubes approaching the city—an army of knights and professional soldiers. We retreated to the ships and turned back for Skarn Harbor.

Of the two hundred men Ragnar had brought along twenty had died. And I knew that twenty wives and many children would never see their husbands and fathers again.

CHAPTER FOURTEEN: BACK TO SKARN

We sailed all the way back to the river, plunder stored beneath our feet. Then, our group of ships broke up. Ragnar headed to Skarn Harbor; King Halfi headed to Hjarthorp; King Hagwine headed to Himnall Hill; and so on. I could hardly keep track of all the names of all the chieftains and villages which dotted Badelgard.

When we reached Skarn Harbor, a very light snow was falling from the dark sky—only a few flakes at a time, melting gently on my cheek. As the night deepened, Ragnar's men and I transported the glistening loot, both gold and silver, from the boats into the Great Hall. The task didn't take much time at all. We piled them up in a corner to be divided amongst us that night.

Inside the Hall, servants stoked the fires furiously to warm the men of Skarn Harbor throughout the icy night. Winter had come, and Boreas the Frost Giant blew his icy breath down from the gods' home in the Dragonteeth; billowing from lofty heights to freeze the helpless villages of mankind.

The women of Skarn Harbor had brewed steaming sweet tea to warm the frigid men.

King Ragnar stood up. "Play us a song, Skadi!" he roared and took a deep gulp of his steaming tea.

A blonde-haired man strummed a lyre as he began to sing a song of the clan's noble ancestry.

According to the bard, many centuries ago a great chieftain named Buntringer and his wife Aelwine were exiled from their home country of Gottarlund. His family wandered the land for months in wintertime until they came to the River Badel, which by then had been frozen solid. There he met and saw with his own eyes the green dragon called Skruga. Buntringer and his sons—Helgur, Himnal and Hjarta—demanded that Skruga leave and allow them to settle in Badelgard. But Skruga refused, and Buntringer fought him for days until they reached the top of the snowy peak called Mount Klaki. There, Buntringer was defeated with one claw-swipe to his head.

But to his great surprise, Skruga then forgave him for his aggression, saying that Buntringer was the mightiest warrior he had ever fought, and the bravest too. Skruga allowed Buntringer to ride upon his scaled back and proceeded to give the entirety of Badelgard to him, allowing his family to drive out the native tribes with his aid. Riding on Skruga, both Buntringer and the Dragon vanished on a journey to reach the Edge of the World. But his descendants lived on.

Helgur and his sons settled near the fjords on the western edge of Badelgard; Himnal and his sons settled in the flat eastern plains; and Hjarta and his sons settled in the wooded north. He then proceeded to give a long genealogy starting with Helgur and branching off into many different clans including that of Skarn Harbor, and eventually proclaiming Ragnar as a royal-blooded descendant and rightful king.

"May Skruga's name be praised!" shouted the king, "Arise, sons of Buntringer! The loot shall be divided like this: each man may take one golden item and four silver items, and fifty silver coins. I have already taken my share."

I saw a large mound of sparkling golden jewelry, and a hoard of silver and golden coins as high as my shoulder, piled up near the throne of Ragnar. A treasure fit for a king.

One by one the raiders sifted through the treasure for what

they thought they needed. When it came to my turn, I had hardly touched the golden candelabra that caught my eye when Ragnar began to shout.

"Alfy can't take any gold. Just take thirty coins. You ain't no son of Buntringer. Am I right, boys?" His men cheered.

After the shock of his statement, I began to shake. My blood ran hot. "How dare you?" I threw the candelabra down with bending force. "I helped you just as much as any of these pigs!"

Inga touched my shoulder but I threw her off me.

"I demand an equal share!"

"You won't get one, by the green scales of Skruga!" Ragnar roared back and raised his axe high.

"You look down on me for my elvish blood, do you?" I said incredulously. "We elves look down on you, and for good reason! We discovered magic, tested and perfected it! We taught you all the arts and sciences. You humans are merely dumb beasts." I paused for a brief second, quaking. "I am not Nocturne. I am Dralynthi Rabaam, son of Drethori and Drassané, from the wealthiest family in Drastheon! By Night Herself, my dad could pay every measly farthing you're worth and sell you as a slave!"

"Nocturne!" Inga shouted, "Snap out of it! Just accept it— you don't get an equal share, yet! Yet! When you've proven yourself, you'll—"

I tuned her out. "Give me an equal share, or I won't help you anymore!" I felt my fangs extend. I looked at the pink, pink neck of Ragnar and ran my tongue around my fangs. Behind that skin was blood—fresh, warm red blood flowing like a river. Red, red blood.

"If you like your home so much, Alfy, why don't you go back, an' never return? We don't need you here amongst the Sons of Buntringer!"

This pushed me well over the edge—partly because I felt

betrayed and partly because I remembered that I could not go back, that I was not accepted by my own people, the elves. I belonged to no one. I could have cried. Instead, I chose to act.

I leapt for Ragnar, climbed upon him with all fours, and sank my teeth deep into his neck. The high, after all these years of withholding, was the greatest I had ever remembered. For the span of ten seconds my mind was in a state of ecstasy indescribable to any who has not experienced it. And I wanted more.

But I wasn't halfway through when I felt the presence of someone behind me. I detached my fangs, and narrowly dodged the hard stroke of an axe, which landed crushingly on Ragnar's wooden throne. Inga cried and screamed.

The Hall was up in arms and I knew I could have struck each one of them dead. But I chose not to. I grabbed *Dreské* and *Dreské* and ran outside into the cold night, into the sweet, sweet darkness that I knew so well.

I ran across the river, and about two miles away from Skarn Harbor I collapsed and began to weep. I cried and cried until I had no tears left; and when I had finally stopped, I fell asleep.

When I awoke I had discarded Nocturne the Sensitive; I had become Nocturne the Monster. For the next three months I completely gave in to bloodlust. I attacked travelers on Badelgard's many roads as winter deepened over the land. I did terrible things— horrible things that should never be even contemplated—that I have since tried to forget. Every impulse I had I gave into, because nothing mattered, and anything that gave me temporary relief would do. Lust and desire for blood were my only passions for three months, and I unleashed both furiously onto the delicate humans of Badelgard.

Then, feeling utterly devastated and hopeless,

contemplating suicide but not really ready to give in, I headed north towards the frozen wastes, toward the Elf Lands; knowing full well that nothing awaited me there.

CHAPTER FIFTEEN: HOUSE OF HORRORS

I traveled for over two months.

When I saw the walls of Naremon in the distance, so bleak and gray, I knew that the capital of Londor would not cure my despair. I knew full well that what had happened long ago might well happen again. Perhaps Madiré's skeleton guards were still searching the city for me, combing through every forest in the country. Perhaps they had discovered the secret of the Waning Crescent Inn, and had thrown all the druen there into the Amphitheatre for the sadistic pleasure of Madiré.

But perhaps I was just thinking too hard. I had walked across the vast expanse of the Elf Lands, from the wild pine forests on the edge of Umdar, across the tame farms and cities of Lamdar, and deep into the dark, brambly wilderness of Londor; I had gone slowly, walking and riding. On the way I had given in to my bloodlust whenever the opportunity arose, but the brief euphoria was ultimately unfulfilling, and when it was over I felt empty inside, as empty as I had been before.

I remembered all the things that went on in the city of Naremon, of my work at the inn and of my forced romance with Queen Madiré. Of the scheming of the hideous crone Marnisi and her efforts to kill me. Of Homar, now long dead. May the gods give his soul rest.

And I also remembered Dead Kings Bluff, the great cliff overlooking the city, and its bloody history as the dying place of so many princes and kings. And in the cool, gray-skied spring morning, I resolved to throw myself off the precipice, and end the meaningless nothingness my life had become.

The hike to Dead Kings Bluff would exhaust me, and it would take every last drop of energy I had. But I knew full well that it would be the only cure to my pain. One step off the bluff, and it would all be over.

I set out at once, climbing the steep Normallen Peak. By the time I had almost reached the precipice, I was sweating heavily and wondering whether I would go on. But I knew I would. It was worth it.

Under my breath I whispered something to Katrina: "Today I join you in Paradise."

But when I had almost had my hands on the wet rock of Dead Kings Bluff, I heard the crackling of a bonfire burning below the cliff itself, in a sheltered valley. Huddled around the fire were four men dressed in long black cloaks. Their faces were grim in the dim light of the fire. Five brown horses sat beside them. I thought nothing of them and started to pull myself up, to leap to my death, when I heard one of them shout to me, "Hey! Hey! Elf!"

Surprised, I let myself fall, and I underestimated the height. My legs hit the pebbly ground hard. Fire surged through my bones and I cursed.

I turned to the men around the bonfire. "What is it?" I hissed.

Then a smile slowly crossed my lips—perhaps I would have one last blood meal before I died. Perhaps I would have an enjoyable last dinner.

"Come over to us, please! We've got something to tell you."

I carefully dislodged my foot from the loose rock, hearing pebbles crunch under my feet, and slowly scooted to the side, around the cliff and into the sheltered area below the bluff. There, the men were staring at me from the bonfire. I noticed that all four were humans. I sneered at them because of this, and having found my footing, I made my way over quickly. "What is so important that you had to interrupt?" I said when I was within speaking range.

One of them got up and stepped forward. He lowered his black hood slowly, revealing a fat face with a large brown moustache and a thick beard. "I am Brother Maven," he said, his voice low, "We sense greatness in you, elf. Are you one of the Fallen Elves—the Blood Drinkers? The Accursed Ones?"

"What is it to you?" I growled and let my fangs extend. I hissed lightly for effect.

"Oh, heavens!" Maven said in ecstasy, "You are a son of Gilden. Great God, you must come with us at once!" He turned to his friends. "He is a son of Gilden, brothers!"

They all looked at me delightedly and stood up from their places around the fire. I returned their affection with a mean snarl. "Why should I come?" I hissed, "What good is in it for me?" "If you come with us," Maven said, "I promise you life eternal. I promise you brotherhood in our service to the only being we give the title 'God.' This is what I promise you, Son of the Night." He reached toward me and I cast his arm away.

"I do not want life eternal," I said, "And neither do I believe in any god. And I do not believe that anyone should be called a god."

Instead of backing off like I wished, my words seemed to excite Maven.

"Oh, you will make a great servant, in time," the chubby man squealed, "Come with us. Do not kill yourself; your life is too valuable in the eyes of our lord."

"How did you know I was going to—"

"The cliff called Dead Kings Bluff is the dying place of many. And I sense your despair; your life is without meaning. Come with us and perhaps one day you may dine amongst our eternal family. And we still have Brother Thomlyn's gelding—you can ride that."

I would have blindly followed any hope to give my life purpose and save myself from destruction. In despair I accompanied Brother Maven and his three followers on their travels along the roads for a period of five days. We would walk all day on road or off, then spend the night over the fire, roasting squirrels or rabbit or whatever meat we could find along the way. Maven was a good shot with the sling.

Around the fire they raved on and on about their newfound lord, but they would not name Him. The intensity of their devotion was bizarre to an uninitiated man such as I. They told me that they had been doing their "lord's service" in the country of the Lonen Elves, traveling to Naremon to receive a report from officials in the area and deliver it to one "Father Grimalvin" in "Cair Avon," which I assumed was where we were headed.

Some time on the eleventh day we arrived at the edge of a crystal clear lake surrounded by trees. In the center of the lake was an island, and on the island I could see a stone castle, built in older style with square towers and very little decoration. Perhaps many centuries ago, it had been a great citadel, a bastion of safety in a dangerous land. But now it was just a residence, a summer home for some rich lord.

"Here is Cair Avon," Brother Maven said, the rolled-up report held tightly in his hand, "Built upon beautiful Goose Lake in Northern Gallia."

The late spring day was gentle and warm, and the trees had all sprouted green leaves. Shrubs sprouted in the underbrush and the verdant scenery sent an exhilarating chill up my spine.

But shouting soon broke up the enjoyment of the scene. A man was paddling a boat towards us.

"Greetings, Brother Maven!" the boatman hollered and pulled up to the sandy beach.

"Greetings, Brother," Maven said.

"Who is this face I do not recognize?" he said.

"This is Nocturne Rabaam. Take a good look; you'll be getting to know that face very well in the future. You see, Nocturne is a Son of Gilden."

The cultist's eyes bulged in delight. "How wonderful! Now come, get inside and I'll paddle you to Cair Avon."

I questioned my judgment severely as I took a step in the boat. I had trusted my life—broken as it was—with these strangers. But my life was worthless to me anyway.

Maven pounded hard on the castle doors with the brass knockers. He turned to me as he waited. "This castle was donated to the Brotherhood by the Sarnoff family. They grew very wealthy in the lumber trade, I believe, and own a number of houses, I believe, throughout this area. Baron Raschard Sarnoff was intrigued by the Brotherhood and the values it taught, and being greatly interested in philosophy, eventually became a Brother. He donated the basement to our cause, thinking that perhaps the Galiopeans wouldn't be ready to embrace such a new, radical philosophy."

"Did I ask you to tell me the history of the castle?" I sneered. My hands reflexively curled into fists and I so desperately wanted to hit him across the jaw.

But he kept prattling on as if I had said nothing. "But you see, the Galiopeans and the higher ups, they do not understand the Brotherhood. They persecute us and have tried to find the location of our headquarters in Cair Avon for the past two years, in an effort to destroy it."

I snapped. "Damn it!" I screamed, grabbing him by the

shoulders and digging my nails hard into his skin. "Tell me what the cult is about or I'll force it out of you."

Maven glanced at me. "The Dark Brethren serve a timeless being who has tried to bring justice to Varda for ages. He appeared once, in his first incarnation, a thousand years ago."

"Name him!" I screamed. I put my hands around his throat. I might have lost control at that second had Maven's followers not moved to restrain me.

"Inquiry is good," he said. "I will not hinder your questioning. You have traveled with us many days now and you deserve an answer. And an answer I will give you. Seymus."

"What?" Seymus was the king of evil, the lord of the damned. The forefather of the vampires, Gilden, sided with him during the War of Shadow; one of many reasons for the Vampire's Curse.

"You bastard," I growled in a voice deep and low. I could feel anger coming onto me like a gathering storm; I hated Maven so deeply, and I wasn't sure why. "You bottom-feeding mongrel."

"Give us a chance, Nocturne," Maven said. "I sense much greatness in you."

The door opened, and Maven's men forced me into the dark castle.

We descended a set of mucky steps, plagued by the constant drip of the ceiling. Those five minutes seemed like an hour to me as my heart began to beat faster and I wondered whether I had made the right choice; whether there was an easier way to die. Whether I truly wanted to die at all.

Finally, we got to the end of the stairs. In the flickering illumination of the torches I saw

upon a metal stake a rotting human head, frozen in an

eternal, silent scream.

I gasped, then choked. A wave of nausea swept over me, and I covered my mouth and gagged down vomit.

"What's wrong? It is a natural object," Maven said. "There is nothing wrong with nature."

My heart was pounding like a drum.

"It is just a bit of decorative art," Maven continued. "Baron Raschard believes it sets the mood for entry—eye candy, if you will." I tried to run but Maven's three men restrained me, holding me by the arms, and kept my hands firmly behind my back as they led me on.

"Now in this room we have Doctor Frederick Sarnoff—he's Baron Raschard's son—working on one of his patients. I think one of them has been naughty. Oh, yes, very naughty, apparently."

Inside the tiny chamber, a long-haired man was operating on a victim, gagged and strapped to a chair. Frederick was even dressed in a physician's outfit, with a woolen cone cap and spectacles.

I struggled to break the men's hold, but their grip was iron strong. I whimpered.

"Oh, hush now," Maven said, "Don't be scared. He isn't as rotten as you think he is. Frederick doesn't only punish—don't worry. Sometimes he rewards."

Finally we reached a square stone chamber lit by braziers placed in all four corners. In the center of the room was a four-foot pile of bones, which I guessed were human or elven in origin. By this point I cared for nothing except escape. I struggled wildly but I just could not break their hold.

"Now here is the center stage of Cair Avon, the Summoning Chamber. For ten years we have prepared the ritual for ushering Seymus back into the world. It is nearly complete. And we want you to join us, Nocturne, in our glory." Maven smiled. "Do not worry; we did not bring you here to be harmed. You will not be our sacrifice; you are a guest in our home. That is not our way; we are decent and honorable folk."

"I can see that."

"So what do you say, Nocturne? Will you become a brother? I sense such great things from you!"

A few hooded figures appeared, armed with maces.

"Yes," I said. They released me.

I had lied. I was a druen, but I would not join my forefather, Gilden, in his greatest mistake. I would never kneel at the feet of the Dark One.

Suddenly I heard a commotion coming from another room—clattering pots and pans and loud squeals.

"Aha, Baron Raschard has come to join us," Brother Maven said, "What a pleasant surprise."

Out of the door a strange figure appeared. The lower half of its body was that of a very fat human. But its head was clearly porcine, with a snout and beady black eyes and coarse, hairy skin. He was squealing loudly and his open mouth revealed tiny blackened teeth. I could see scraps of flesh in its mouth, not yet digested, and he stank of rot. Had he dined on one of Frederick's "patients?"

Maven turned to the monster. "Oh, Baron, are you out of food?" he said. His eyes turned towards me. "Don't be afraid of him. We made a mistake with one part of our ritual, that's all. We were supposed to sacrifice a pig... but Baron Raschard became joined with swine. It's quite fine. Raschard's quite a gentleman, even if he looks and acts a bit—shall I say—porcine?"

Heart pounding, I turned and sped down the hallway, feeling like I wanted to vomit, running faster than I had in my life. In that moment I could have lifted a wagon or run a hundred miles. I pushed past the cultists so forcefully that they hit the wall.

I charged up the stairs, but the cultists chased after me. I ran until I came to the doors, threw them open, and dashed outside. I could hear their footsteps getting louder and louder in my ears.

Out in the open air a cultist dashed near me as I struggled in the boat. I set off, but he leapt on deck. The cultist, carrying a massive iron-spiked mace, thumped me hard on the head with his weapon. I could feel the blood rushing. Feeling dizzy, I somehow managed to throw him into the water.

I rowed back to the mainland as I bled, slowly losing my wits.

I got out of the boat clumsily. I ran as long and far as I could, but I could feel blood pouring from my head and down my back. The blood was soaking my shirt and trousers. I was losing my energy. I knew I was going to die.

I do not remember much after that, and what I do remember is fuzzy and blended all together. I ran until the forest became a plain, and the plain became an orchard, and the orchard became a field of rolling wheat. And I swear that during that journey I saw Katrina running through the woods, like a white-garbed nymph in some fantastical children's tale. And her face was bright, so bright, as I collapsed into the soft blanket of wheat. So bright indeed…

I was soaked with blood—drenched, even—and I could feel it caked to my head. I knew full well that I was going to die… but at least I had seen Katrina.

My vision faded, and I knew I was no more.

CHAPTER SIXTEEN: KITTY

I felt the sensation of a cool, wet cloth dabbing at my eye. My head was throbbing and I could feel blood running down my nose. Then the moist cloth wiped the blood away.

Someone was pouring water down my throat—no, milk. I choked and spat some out. I felt like throwing up.

Silence. Sweet, sweet, silence.

Then someone started playing with my eyelids.

I heard a voice, though it all seemed unreal to me in my half-sleep. "Oh, ain't he handsome?" it said. It was a girl's voice. "He's out of a dream. Look at his eyes! Those brilliant blue eyes. They're like ice floatin' in a river!"

An older, harsh voice. "Don't have improper thoughts now, Kitty. I didn't have one impure thought before I married your Granddaddy. And you better believe it's a fact."

"Oh, I believe you, Granny."

The dreamlike vision faded.

The next thing my eyes beheld was the face of a young woman. Her eyes were brown, the color of a chestnut, and her many locks of hair were reddish in color. Her lips were curved, thin and pink, and her cheeks were rosy, pink and flushed. She was human.

I wanted to speak to her. But I could hardly move.

"Are you awake?" she asked.

As I scooted upright, pain filled my head. My blurry vision slowly cleared and I observed my surroundings. I was in a beautiful house, in a living room with wooden floor and a bear hide rug, a couch and a table. I had been lying on a straw mattress, with a hard-packed pillow to support my head.

I caught a fleeting vision of myself in the glass window. There was slight bruising under my eyes and my hair looked very disheveled. That mace must have done some serious damage to my skull. And speaking of my skull, the back of my head was throbbing like a drum.

It was very warm inside. Wonderfully warm. It was summer. And a tiny baby was crawling around on the floor, dressed in miniature clothing.

I looked beside me. By the mattress was a bowl of hot chicken broth and a huge glass of ice cold milk. "Yes," I answered finally. It hurt a bit to speak, and my mouth was dry. I wanted to grab that milk, but I was afraid I would be too weak. "Yes. I'm awake."

"What's your name? I've been wondering ever since we found you!"

"D-Dralynthi… err, I mean Nocturne. Yes, yes, Nocturne."

"Nocturne? What a beautiful name!" the girl said in an excited voice that reminded me of a naïve eleven-year-old girl, even though she was clearly somewhere around twenty. She had a ribbon in her hair, and she smelled like flowers. Perhaps it was some perfume she had applied.

I struggled to give her a weak smile, though my head was throbbing hard.

"What is *your* name?" I stammered. Speaking was an effort in itself.

She blushed, as if she were shocked that anyone would ever ask her such a question. "My name is Kitty Coy," she said, "Well my real name is Kitteryn but everyone seems to like calling me Kitty."

I wanted to lie down. That chicken broth looked good.

"I'm glad you're up," Kitty said, "Granny Coy has baked a nice apple pie." The thought of eating pie right now made me sick. "Oh, she makes the best apple pies in the whole wide world, I swear it!" she continued. "We also have a great bottle of wine from vineyards! Do you like white wine, Nocturne?"

"I prefer it," I lied.

"My mother never let me have a drop until I was sixteen. She's a prude, I tell you! And hey—Edwin!—get that thing out of your mouth."

The baby was biting the head off a woolen doll. Kitty marched over to him, reached down a forceful hand and snatched it away. The baby began crying pitifully—tears and all.

"Oh, you're incorrigible, Edwin! How many times have I told you not to be cruel to dolls?" After a while her voice turned from anger to sympathy. She just couldn't be mean to it.

"Oh, sweet baby," she said, cradling him tightly in his arms. She gave him tiny kisses until he stopped his tears. "I'm sorry, Edwin." When the baby was silent, she turned toward me and said. "He's my sister Joan's baby. She and my brother-in-law are visiting family in Galiope, and they don't want to scare poor Edwin with all the sounds and sights of the big city! So they left him with us."

Galiope. Wasn't that where Katrina was from? Too much thinking.

"Do you mind if I relax a while?" I asked.

"Not at all!" Kitty said, "As long as you're up for dinner! I can't wait for you to meet the family!"

I laid back down, carefully, ever so carefully. And within seconds of shutting my eyes, I relaxed into a very deep sleep.

My next memory was Kitty waking me up again. "Ready to eat dinner?"

"Yes," I lied. I was still very tired.

Slowly, she helped me to my feet and led me clumsily through a hallway and into the dining room. I was exhausted, but I was determined to meet the people who had saved my life.

Dinner had been prepared on the table. Kitty helped ease me into my seat carefully and slowly.

On the table, several lean steaks and a bowl of strawberries had been prepared. The strawberries looked red and ripe. The steaks were cooked well and smelled delicious. But I could not eat tough meat in this state. Thankfully, a bowl of thick brown broth had been placed in front of me, and a cup of milk. But the food at the table was much less interesting than the people sitting around it.

"I'm Bella Coy. It's good to meet you," said a woman with a long brown ponytail and a short, thin, muscular build. I thought her rather pretty.

"I'm Nocturne," I said with a smile.

"I'm Morris Coy, Bella's husband," said a tall, plump man of middle age, with balding brown hair. Many years on the farm had given him such a strong physique, I'd guess. I am sure if we got into a match of fisticuffs he would take me down in seconds.

"And I'm Saria," said a friendly-looking old woman with long white hair done in a ponytail. Granny Coy.

Kitty was there also, and baby Edwin in his highchair.

"It's nice to meet all of you," I said.

It seemed strange to me that a vampire—a ruthless predator—should be dining with such kind-hearted people, as if the thought that I might defile his daughter never occurred to Mr. Coy. But I had never been one to refuse an invitation. And to them, I was just an elf. I doubted they knew the telltale marks of a druen.

"So where are you from, Nocturne?" Morris Coy said as he grabbed a steak and began cutting into it with a knife. He shoveled the bits of meat into his mouth as he cut it.

I thought about this deeply for a second, realizing I really had no idea. "From Naremon," I said. It was not a lie, because there was no true answer.

Morris looked at me sharply. "I don't know where that is," he said matter-of-factly, "Sounds elvish. And that's what you are—elvish. Right?"

I nodded.

"There's a lot of you folks in the city," he said, "Not so many in the country."

I looked at him in surprise. A human city, with an elven population?

"What were you doing when we found you?" Morris said, "You were half dead, sprawled in the wheat crop, when Kitty stumbled upon you. Gods' sakes, you were bleeding from your head. You're lucky we were there in time."

I took a deep gulp of water. "Well it is a long story," I said, "A very, very long story."

"We've got time!" Bella said cheerfully.

I began with my exploits in Badelgard, a nation very distant and exotic to them, a land which they believed was filled with red-bearded raiders riding on dragons and other imaginative fancies. I had to correct many of the false ideas they had fostered. Mr. Coy seemed especially disappointed by the fact that Badelgarders don't actually ride on dragons.

I did tell most of the story, but I left out the part about the raiding of Stormhold, fearing it would offend such naïve and goodhearted folk, but did tell them of the Badelgarder's rejection of me, and how I was forced to leave.

Kitty frowned. "Well they obviously hadn't very good tastes, Nocturne."

I smiled. "Thank you."

"Them Badelgarders are a rough lot," Morris added, "I'm surprised they didn't kill you first off and steal all your silver. Those raiders are good for nothing but fighting, I'll tell you. The king of Zarubain's been trying to stop them from their dirty habits for years. No such luck, however."

I smiled and felt strangely warm. For a second I believed that there were humans who were kind. I continued the story, with my wanderings back to Naremon, leaving out my attempts at suicide, and lied, telling them that the cultists kidnapped me rather than that I went willingly. Leaving out the most disturbing of the horrors I witnessed at Cair Avon, I told them of my escape and my injured flight to the edge of the Coy Farm.

"That's horrible!" Kitty said, "Some people are just rotten, I tell you!"

"Rotten is an understatement," I said with a smile. I took my spoon and drank some of the hot, salty chicken broth.

We soon finished our dinners and only a few strawberries remained. Outside the sky had gone dark and a refreshingly cool wind blew in from the open window.

"Tomorrow do you want to make yourself useful and help milk the cows?" Morris asked.

"I'd love to, Mr. Coy," I said. "I've not been feeling myself, but perhaps tomorrow that will change."

The farmer smiled and nodded. "Let's hope so."

I was given a room up in the attic. The bed I still could not sleep in, lest I fall and injure my head, but we moved the straw mattress from the living room upstairs. The room was quite small, but nice. I had my own window staring out into the beautiful fields and forests, and Morris opened it for me to let in the cool air.

The wooden floors were dusty, and I'd wish for more

space, but tonight would be a very, very nice rest and I would certainly have sweet dreams. Morris helped me onto the mattress and then left.

I shut my eyes in total relaxation. As sleep overcame me, I smiled. The Coys were nice and good-hearted. But whether they would stay kind, or whether they would reject me like the other humans I'd known, I wasn't sure.

I awoke very early in the morning.

Morris Coy was hunched over me, poking my shoulder to get me to wake up. The sky was dark and the sun had not yet arisen.

My head still hurt, and I couldn't touch my eyes because of the bruising, but I was determined to help Mr. Coy with the cows and pay him back for saving my life.

He led me down the stairs and out of the house, and we walked a while in the cool morning air to the barn. He had already locked the cows in position. He handed me a dented milk pail. Moving slowly, I scooted it underneath the cow's udders.

"Have you milked a cow before, Nocturne?" he asked.

I couldn't shake my head without pain. "No," I said simply, "I haven't, Mr. Coy. Do you care to explain?"

"Grab an udder in each hand, like so. You squirt one, the other recharges, you squirt the other. Begin at the top of the udder and slide your fingers down, like it's a tube."

I ran my fingers down the cow's pink udders one by one and watched the cow's milk squirt into the pail little by little. The cow occasionally groaned and I wondered if I was doing something wrong, but Morris said I wasn't.

After a few squirts I got a handle on it and started milking the cow at a reasonable rate, although Mr. Coy finished well before me. Soon the pail was full to the brim with cool white milk.

I stood up, lifting my bucket in my hand, and gave the cow a pat on the back as her furry tail slapped at flies. She groaned loudly.

"You did well," Morris said with a smile, and patted me on the back. I returned his smile with one of my own.

"Thank you," I said.

But his soft expression was short lived, and soon turned gruff and businesslike. After all, I was the farmer's apprentice. "Now we take the milk back to the house. And be nice 'n careful not to spill."

I recovered at a slow pace. By the middle of Brenua, I was up on my feet and able to help Morris Coy. One day I awoke to see that the bruising around my eyes had vanished. Eventually, the pain in my head went away as well, and I once again felt myself. I was able to run, jump, and lift heavy objects without any pain whatsoever.

I helped Morris around the farm by day, and by night I would stay in the company of Kitty as she took care of baby Edwin. Slowly, very slowly, day by day, Kitty began to become prettier and prettier to me—not that she hadn't been beautiful before. But soon as got to know her, she became a goddess, the ideal woman. Sometimes she reminded me of Katrina—her voice, her hair, her beauty and her quiet confidence.

One day in early summer, Kitty's older sister Joan and her husband Luther returned from the city and took Edwin back to their home a couple miles away in the town of Bandon. Joan looked rather like her sister Kitty, with curly auburn hair and a tall, lean body. Luther was thin and not so muscular, but the fact that he was a shoemaker probably explained it.

During the month of Aurelios I helped Morris shear his

sheep. The lumps of wool would sell for four shillings apiece, and the sheep were Morris's most profitable animals besides the cows. Collecting eggs was also a chore, but they were very useful in Bella's cooking. Morris's wife knew a thousand ways to cook eggs.

The time for harvesting hay would come late in the month or in early Odens, depending on the weather, and after that we still had the wheat harvest to worry about. A farmer's work was never done.

For the first time in my life I felt like a real man of the earth, and there was something so much more natural about earning a living this way than by raiding, crafting, or hawking wares. I got dirty every day, and didn't always have the time to wash. I stank, and I was filthy, but by dinnertime, I knew I had earned every morsel of food on my plate.

One hot night after work, when sweat slicked my white skin, Morris and I were sitting in the living room with tall mugs of milk. I had begun to trust the Coys just a bit more. I began my story again, intending to leave in the parts that I had previously thought unsuitable.

I started with Katrina all those years ago, how I had fallen in love with her after saving her from Dreddani, how I had run off with her, and how she had eventually died because of my great foolishness. And that was when Morris stopped me with a look of surprise on his face.

"Do you remember Katrina's last name?" the balding man asked.

"I believe it was Stanbridge," I answered.

For a moment Morris just looked at me in shock. "Katrina Stanbridge disappeared around two decades ago," he said, sounding mystified, "I was eight years her elder and knew her pretty well. I remember her parents thought she ran away. She never returned. And you're saying she was sold into slavery? Into the Elf Lands? I thought surely she had been killed by wolves, or bears, or bandits. But she died—"

"By my hands."

"Don't blame yourself, Nocturne," Morris said, "You, if anything, gave her a chance of salvation."

I let his words sink in a while. Perhaps it was true, that if I hadn't been there she would have died. But still, if we hadn't gone into Sardur she'd still be alive. "Can you tell me more about her family?" I asked.

"The Stanbridge Vineyards make some of the finest wine in the whole region. They import it all over the Northlands, and some folks say it's as good as Zarube varieties. Stanbridge Wine is white. It has a nice, crisp and sweet taste. Very blunt," Morris said, "I believe Uther Stanbridge died suddenly a few years ago. Marian is deathly sick and bedridden. They took her disappearance hard, I tell you. Somehow they blamed themselves."

"I'd better give her mother the news," I said melancholically, "She deserves to know. Do you know where Marian lives?"

Morris nodded. "I'll take you there, once we get a good break from the work. The ride is very quick by horse."

Somehow I felt reassured by the fact that they knew Katrina, that somehow, beyond death, there was a small piece remaining in the memories she had left behind. Some of her kin were still alive, some of her flesh and blood, and I would be her messenger.

CHAPTER SEVENTEEN: THE JEWEL OF THE NORTH

One hot day, Morris and I tossed the burlap sacks of wool in a carriage and started off on a journey to the city of Galiope. The horses pulled us fast down the dirt packed road, but as we got closer to the city proper the roads became paved with stone; harder on the horseshoes but easier on the feet.

I was very excited to see a large human city. Of course I had been to Skarn Harbor—but I considered Skarn more a tiny village, if even that—and I knew some human clans had much bigger settlements than the Badelgarders. Some human cities rivaled even Naremon or Danarion in size.

We left in the early hours of the morning and arrived sometime just as noon struck in Galiope's great clock tower. I could hear the church bells ringing throughout the streets. As we got closer I saw that the curtain wall surrounding Galiope was very high, and wide at the top to allow for fighting, with archers posted at all times.

The main southern gatehouse was called Godsgate. We paid the gatekeeper a toll of one silver penny, and Morris and I were subsequently allowed in.

We had made it only a few steps in when the farmer said, "Why don't you have fun and explore a bit, and I'll go take care of selling the wool?"

I nodded. "I'll do that, Morris. Thanks."

Naturally I proceeded straight down High Street, the main cobbled road that pierced the heart of the city. Immediately north of Godsgate was Cathedral District, Galiope's religious quarter. I saw many grim churches and temples of white limestone to various human gods, intermixed with clusters of sprawling, dirty townhouses and shops. I could see people of every kind walking up and down the avenue—elves, from Umen to Lamen; humans from both north and south; thick-bearded Iron Dwarfs and clean shaven Forest Dwarves; ratlings; crooks and pickpockets; rich men; young purple-garbed schoolboys; and hooded priests singing their evening chants.

Eventually a great stone bridge over the river came into view, and after that I could see Midtown, Galiope's main stretch of shops and entertainment—the Civic Arena and the Racetrack among them. And though I felt a bit awkward as a newcomer, no one looked at me strangely. It was a human city, yes, but it had elves as well, of every tribe. Cities in the Elf Lands were almost always homogeneously elven. I wondered whether there were a few druen here too.

I glanced to my right and saw a shady area of town. My heart leapt as I realized the architecture was elven—and not only elven, but of the Lonen Tribe, like that of Naremon. The roofs of the houses were elegantly curved and shingled in bright purple, with luminous glass windows that amplified the candlelight therein. And walking the cobbled streets of that district were people like me—elves with dark hair and white, corpselike skin. In excitement I turned towards it and began down a winding narrow path.

Two steps in I noticed a beautiful black-haired woman dallying nearby. She was leaning on the whitewashed wall of a house. A half-finished bottle of red wine was in her hand. "What is this place?" I asked her politely.

Her voice was raspy and gruff for a woman. "This is Lonen

Town, silly," she said, "You not from these parts?" Her eyes were sharp and feline.

"Why, no," I said, "I've never been in human lands before—or a human city, at least."

"Then you may very well fit in, this side of town," she said, then switched her tongue to elvish. "Half the people in Lonen Town can't speak a word of Galiopean."

I smiled. "Sounds like my kind of place."

"You doing something important?" she said. "I can show you around."

"No," I said, "Not at all. I've got time."

We walked a while down the winding path. As we progressed, I noticed the buildings were getting shabbier and shabbier. I guessed we were heading toward a slum.

Then she stopped. "Here is the Bloodmoon Inn," she said, pointing to a building crammed between two tenement houses. The tenements were rather hideous to behold—one was painted a ghastly, lurid yellow; the other a flaky green. The least the owners could do was take care of their homes, but for some lesser elves, I suppose that was just simply too much to ask.

The inn between the tenements was very tall but rather narrow, using all the space it could manage without violating city laws. A thick coat of red paint was swathed over the wood; and as a whole, the inn did not seem as dilapidated as the rest of the seedy eyesores nearby. On the door, a wooden placard read in elvish: "The Bloodmoon Inn & Tavern."

A fat elven man stepped out of the inn to greet us. He had a large, sagging potbelly and his black hair was slightly balding. "Why hello." He set down a wet cloth on the doorknob to clasp my guide's hand, then kissed hers gently. Realizing there was another, third presence, he turned his head to face me. "And who is this, Madame?"

"Nocturne," I said, "Nocturne Rabaam."

"I am Omagon Naron," the elf said, "I run the Bloodmoon."

"A pleasure to make your acquaintance," I said politely and gave him a slight bow.

"Good manners, he's got. Is he moving in here, Dray?" Omagon asked my guide. He spat a bit of food out of his mouth and onto the street. "If so I might need an extra cook around here. You cook, Nocturne?"

"I do," I said, "I like to think I'm quite good at it actually. I used to work at the Waning Crescent in Naremon."

Omagon's eyes glinted in surprise.

"However, I don't plan on moving here," I explained, "Not right now, at least. Lovely neighborhood, though. If I ever do decide to live in Galiope, I'll certainly let you know."

"Always need more workers at the Bloodmoon," Omagon said, "Well, it was nice to meet you. Always nice to meet a fellow elf."

The pudgy man ducked back through the doors into his inn, grabbing the cloth on the way out. The next item "Dray" showed me was a large stained-glass cathedral made of stone. It was in a rare break in the clogged mass of sprawling tenements and shanties, having a large open stone courtyard and ample space for visitors to walk about. A few Lonen Elves dallied outside its massive double doors.

The front rose window depicted a Lonen Elf being hanged, and a throng of other elves kneeling before him in worship. The glasswork was beautiful, with bright celestial blues and ruby reds that dazzled the eye in the sunlight. The masonry was also extremely ornate, and two vivid statues of hooded elves guarded the double doors.

"This is the Saint Mortagg Cathedral," the woman said, "There are two stories that claim why it was built, and they don't match up. The humans say a Lonen Elf named Mortagg burned down Lonen Town in year 620 after losing a gambling match, then he killed a city councilman in a drunken rage. And he was hanged for that. But we elves know better. The city councilman set Lonen Town on fire, Saint Mortagg killed him in defense of his people, and he was executed for doing the right thing. He was a martyr. A martyr very deserving of a cathedral." She smiled at me. "When the Queen of Londor heard of this grievous breach of conduct, she donated a thousand marks to the building of this wonder. Several nobles also donated, from East Arloma and such, and we elves managed to construct it without much opposition from the Council. The human citizens though, they didn't much like it, but we defended it against their vandalism until they accepted its existence."

I nodded. "I thought cathedrals were a piece of human architecture, though, usually."

"Yes," she said, "But we are elves in human lands, and we *have* adopted a few—very few—things of theirs that we like. And you have to admit, this Cathedral is beautiful!" She paused and turned to me. She was gorgeous but fierce—a sleek, beautiful panther that might play with you a while and then eat you up. "Now would you like to see some more?" she asked.

"I've got to get back to the person I came with," I said, "But it was a pleasure to meet you as always, Dray. Is that your real name, or a nickname?"

A knowing grin overtook her face. A fanged grin. "My real name is Drassané," she said.

"Why, that's my mother's name," I said, "And that's not Lonen… that's Druenic!"

She opened her mouth and hissed, letting her fangs extend in clear view. She was a vampire. "And you are too," she said, "I can tell just from your smell."

"So it's legal for us to be here?"

"No," Drassané said, "But it's easy to keep a secret from these ignorant folk."

I laughed lightly. "I've got to go. But it was nice to meet you, Drassané."

I found Mr. Coy back at Godsgate, where he explained he had booked a room at an inn in the Midtown district. The walk there was nice, and even in the night Galiope was quite active. Musicians lined the streets—drummers, flutists and pipers—not to mention acrobats and fire eaters desperate for coin.

We awoke early the next morning and headed back to the farm on our carriage. My time in Galiope was very well spent. I had felt very welcome there, and by the time the farmhouse was in sight, I had already promised myself I would return to that city someday to live, permanently.

CHAPTER EIGHTEEN: THE MESSENGER

Out of the window one morning, I saw the grass in the hayfields had grown long, but not yet long enough to be harvested.

The air was hot and muggy as Morris Coy and I set out for the Stanbridge Vineyards. I planned to inform Katrina's mother of her daughter's fate, though I was seventeen years late. Poor old Marian Stanbridge deserved to know.

We sweated through our tunics and trousers in the heat. We rode swiftly past fields of wheat and beans. We cut through apple orchards and small untamed spurts of woodland. The scent of wildflowers hung strong in the air, filling our noses with nature's most intoxicating fragrance.

Rural Gallia was so beautiful in the summer; a quaint, pastoral beauty you could never find in the stony gloom of Naremon or Varda's other big cities. The air was fresh and unclogged by the smoke of blacksmiths and the unbearable stench of tanneries, and the deer ran wild.

We made it to the Vineyards in very good time just as Morris had said. The grapes were still unripe on the leafy green vines. A few tan children were playing outside with wooden swords, imagining themselves to be knights or men at arms.

The Stanbridge house was constructed with heaping stones, with a beautiful brown-shingled roof and an elegant redbrick chimney. We walked up to the door.

Morris knocked firmly and waited.

A golden-haired young man answered. "Yes?" he said politely, "What is it?"

"I would like to see Marian Stanbridge," I said.

He looked at me with a combination of interest and fear, noticing my elvish features in surprise. I guessed they were not used to seeing elves out in the country.

"She is very sick," the man said, "What is it about?"

"It's very important," I said, "It's about Katrina."

His eyes widened and he paused for a second in shock, mouth agape. "Right this way, good sirs."

Marian was very old and wrinkled, her sparse hair mostly gray. She was lying in bed weakly, the covers pulled tight around her despite the humidity of the house. A pewter glass of wine, half-drunk, sat on her bedside table. Perhaps one day before she had grown so old, she had been a beauty.

"Who is there? Is that you, Finn?" she said.

"No," I said, "My name is Nocturne. We haven't met before. But I have met your daughter… Katrina."

"Katrina?" she gasped. I worried that I had startled her, that the shock might be too much for her weak old heart to bear. "What of her?" she continued. "Is she here? Is she alive?"

"No," I said sadly, struggling to retain the austerity of my voice, "She is dead. She died seventeen years ago. But I just wanted to tell you, she died in my arms. She was the most wonderful girl I had ever known. The slavers caught her when she wandered away for a while, when she had reached the Galios River. They sold her into the Elf Lands and eventually she was taken very far away, to my village, Drastheon. I bought her to save her. I sacrificed my status, my life for her, even. I just wanted you to know, I loved your daughter. And that though I am an elf, and unfit to love a human, I thought she was the most wonderful, most beautiful, the strongest girl I have ever known."

A tear ran down Marian Stanbridge's wrinkled, unmoving cheek and down her neck. I walked over and grabbed the edge of the blanket. I dabbed away the tear softly, so very softly.

"Thank you," she managed to say. Her voice was shaking. "Thank you for telling me, Nocturne. I thought that perhaps I would never know what happened to her. Oh, Katrina. Sweet Katrina... we frustrated her. We worked her too hard. We made her run away; she had no choice." Her voice shook and she began to weep. "You may leave me now," she said shakily, "Thank you, Nocturne. Oh, thank you... I am fine to die, now that I know." She paused. "Finn," she said weakly, "Give him a bottle of wine on me, before he goes."

Finn got a bottle of Stanbridge Wine and placed it in my hands. It was the vintage of 1076. A good, well-aged wine.

Morris and I rode back and made the journey before dark. We shared the bottle at dinner, passing it between ourselves with glee. The wine, indeed, was some of the finest I'd ever tasted. Crisp but not harsh; sweet but not overpowering; it was a delight that lasted as long as the bottle, and that did not last long.

Late summer in Galiope was synonymous with the hay harvest, and we spent most of the time taking our scythes to the long-grown grasses, bundling them and letting them dry, and carting the hay indoors for storage. The cows and pigs and horses needed feed for the upcoming winter, and winters in Gallia could be relatively long.

One night, my muscles aching with overuse and my whole body dripping with sweat, I was relaxing in the living room. Unbeknownst to Kitty and her mother, I could hear every word of their conversation as they talked in the kitchen.

"You cannot love an elf, Kitteryn Coy!" Bella snapped sharply at her daughter. "You will marry a nice young human boy, who will take good care of you, and I won't entertain you by listening to your pathetic tirades. Now go to bed. I won't hear of it anymore."

"Mother!" Kitty screamed, almost hissed. I had never seen such fight in her. "I thought you'd at least be understanding. Haven't you ever fallen in love with someone?"

"No," her mother said sternly, "I don't believe in love. I believe in opportunity and circumstance. There is no reason you can't marry a human lad. You should marry Robert Greenleaf— there's a charming young man who knows how to run a farm."

"Robert? Robert is revolting!" Kitty screamed, showing an aggressive side in sharp contrast to her normal meek and cheery demeanor around me. "I don't think he's washed himself in years! I should rip off my skin if that boy ever touched me." She shrieked. "And he is so ugly!"

I thought sadly to myself for a while. Elves did not marry humans, and humans did not marry elves. It would have been a long shot, anyway. We came from such different cultures, incompatible ones.

I was disappointed, yes; but I would not go against Mrs. Coy's wishes.

Sextil meant the wheat harvest. The long stalks had turned dry, brown, and ripe. The heads of wheat rolled in the wind like a sea of amber.

To this day I never remember working so hard in my life. Every day of the month, we arose early and went to bed well after dark. Luckily Bella Coy always had a delicious meal to reward us for the hard work, and hearty meals too—steaks, herb-baked potatoes, and elaborate dishes I had never eaten. And when each day was finished, I felt very proud that I had done a hard day's work and could now enjoy well-earned relaxation in my soft straw bed.

The grain had to be cut with a sickle, and the straw afterwards had to be cut for use in thatching and bed-stuffing. Towards the end of the month Morris noticed how fatigued I was getting, how each day was becoming more and more an immense struggle for me. I was so unused to farm work. By late Sextil I was haggard and exhausted, and wasn't helping much with the harvest.

So about noon on what I believe was the twenty-fifth of Sextil he told me that he wanted me to take a long break until Yule. That meant months of doing nothing, but despite all my protests he refused to allow me to work. He said he had a bit of money stored up and would hire a temporary worker to replace me. Besides, the harvest was over half done.

It was that very day, when I returned to the house wiping sweat from my face with my sleeve, that Kitteryn Coy laid bare her true feelings for me.

"I think I love you, Nocturne."

I said nothing, only looked at her.

I was very attracted to her, yes. But I was very afraid of what her father might say; and I already knew what her mother thought of her daughter loving an elf. I was not about to throw it all away by defying their wishes. Staying amongst these people was healing me inside. They were giving me a reason to live.

"Your parents disapprove," I forced myself to say. "I won't go against their wishes."

Her eyes moistened. "So then, you don't love me?"

I looked at her firmly. "No. I'm sorry, Kitty." I got up and headed back to my attic bedroom to rest my weary bones.

As I did, I could heard her weeping.

But even after that, my feelings didn't leave me. I found myself staring at her, admiring her pretty face; her ripe lips; her soft, glistening hair that fell about her shoulders. She was beautiful, as beautiful as Katrina was, almost twenty years ago. And more than that, she was kind and strong.

And I knew that her feelings did not leave her, either. Occasionally I would notice her staring blankly in my direction, then quickly looking away when our eyes met. She wanted to stay the strong one; she wanted to appear in control. But I could tell she was still in love, despite the fact that she avoided me.

I was firm and unyielding that I would go with Farmer Coy's wishes; staying at their home was giving me reason to keep going day by day, and survive. Before I had come here I had been broken. Now, all these weeks later, I felt at least partially healed.

Harona came, and the air began to cool down ever so slightly.

Wheat farmers such as Morris spent the idle days threshing his wheat, beating the grains away from the chaff and into buckets. Bella used the inedible straw to stuff beds and make hats, a favorite pastime of hers.

It had been a very good harvest, and the Coy family would get through the winter easily. But in the Stanbridge Vineyards and elsewhere, the grape harvest had just begun, and it was their turn to work. Still, the apple harvest had not yet come for those who tended the orchards.

Mr. Coy could settle down before dusk. His mother seemed very happy about his presence, and Kitty's granny had many great stories to share over dinner. She was old—older than me—and could tell many grandiose stories of ancient wars, of the great heroic battles that mankind waged against itself.

Kitteryn and I talked little by little, every once in a great while, but she had hardened her heart against me and she wouldn't forgive me for not loving her. The words she did speak to me always had a trace of bitterness, a hint of acidity hidden deep behind them. No longer was she sweet, meek Kitty, but stubborn and bitter Kitteryn. She would not let me touch her, or sit with her by myself. I did what I could to survive, as always.

Then one day I saw a local boy in the front of the house, reclining with Kitty on a wooden bench on the porch. Their lips touched.

I waited outside the door for minutes. I waited until she came through the door, and then I growled, "Who was that?"

Kitty's eyes met mine with nonchalance. "Does it concern you, Nocturne?"

"Yes," I said, "Who was it?"

"It was Robert Greenleaf. It is my concern alone whom I choose to kiss," she said, "Why do you ask?"

She was getting satisfaction out of the anger I hid.

Autumn caught on. One day, when the leaves had turned red and yellow and orange, and the air was cold and crisp, the Coy family donned their cloaks and set off by coach to a distant village named Bandon. The ride was about ten miles, and took us perhaps four hours by carriage. The roads were hard on the wheels due to the previous day's rain, but we managed to get there before noon.

Bandon I remembered, was the town where Joan and Luther lived. Morris told me it was a town of four hundred, the capital of the shire, and that there we would celebrate the Apple Festival among friends.

The village was sizeable, with two taverns, a large stone church to some obscure harvest goddess named Avelona, a cluster of houses and shops, and a large inn called *Light's Hope Lodge*. Barrels of apples lined the streets and merchants' stands dominated the view, with hard apple cider and apple brandy and apple pies. They were selling every apple product I could imagine, and every apple product I hadn't yet imagined.

Hundreds of people had gathered in town to celebrate, but Farmer Coy had booked rooms in advance at the *Lodge*. We would be staying at Bandon in comfort, although many less prepared revelers would be staying there in squalor.

He had reserved two rooms—one for Kitty and Bella; the other, for him and me.

Mr. Coy and I had two shots of apple brandy at the bar while Kitty and her mother shared a shepherd's pie at a back table. As I tipped the shot glass into my mouth and felt the fiery brandy sear my throat, I couldn't help but notice Kitty glaring at me in between bouts of talking to her mother. She still hadn't gotten past me.

And neither had I gotten past her.

"You know, Nocturne," Morris said, his hot breath smelling of liquor, "I think my daughter's madly in love with you." "Is she?" I felt sorrow deep inside.

"All she keeps blabbering about is how you rejected her, and she's fuming. Silly little girl can't seem to get over you."

"Well I know it isn't okay with you, Morris," I answered, "I know you don't want you daughter to love someone like me."

"What makes you think that?"

"She's innocent," I said, "I'm an elf. And I'm not so innocent. I've done some terrible things, Mr. Coy—"

"Haven't we all, Nocturne?" the farmer said, "We're all bad, every one of us. It's just a matter of circumstances, how much bad we do.”

“So are you saying—if you don’t mind my being so bold—that I can, um…”

“It’s all right with me, Nocturne, if my daughter loves an elf,” Coy said, “You know why?” He signaled the innkeeper to give him another shot of apple brandy. “Because I like you, Nocturne. That’s why.”

A chill ran up my spine. At that second I stood up from the bar, the taste of harsh liquor lingering on my tongue, and walked over to Kitty with confidence. I took her by the hand and led her to her feet. Slowly, as the flutist played his quick-paced melody, we danced. And I kissed her, for the first time.

Over a hot apple pie the next morning, Kitty and I had a long talk.

“That boy you kissed,” I said, “Who was he?”

Kitty laughed uncontrollably, as if her betrayal of me were the funniest thing in the world. “That was Robert. Oh, dear gods, the lengths I went to make you jealous.”

“So you weren’t—”

“Oh, no! Not by Cerne’s green beard! Did you notice how ugly he was?” she said. Then she faked a look of horror. “Am I that ugly?” Kitty laughed. “Why did you tell me you didn’t love me?”

I clasped her hand in mine. “Kitty, I overheard your mother talking. I thought your parents didn’t want us to love each other.”

“They changed their mind over the months,” she said, “When they saw how hard you worked, what a great suitor you would be for me.”

I smiled.

“Shall we enjoy the festivities?” she asked.

“We certainly shall,” I said, and together, holding hands, we got up from the table and our half-finished pie.

The Apple Festival was a great deal of fun, and I spent almost all of my time with Kitty. For a brief period I was happier than I had ever been, than I had ever remembered being in my entire life.

I participated in the apple throwing contest, and Kitty and I won second prize. I bobbed for apples in the ice cold water. I was a contestant in the pie eating contest, though I lost in the first round. And I voted Kitty to be the Apple Queen, though she didn't win.

To this day, memories of the Apple Festival of 1106 burn fresh in my mind. I remember that Kitty and I were happy. I remember, for the first time, that Kitty and I had truly fallen in love.

The following month, we butchered a pig to get us through the upcoming winter. Winters in Galiope were long—they didn't last an eternity like Drastheon or Naremon—but still, a considerable amount of snow lay on the ground for a long time.

Temperatures were unbearably cold for frail, unprotected human bodies. Luckily, we all had the weeklong Feast of Yule to look forward to on the twentieth of Candlebright.

CHAPTER NINETEEN: NEW HOPE

The air grew steadily colder as the days went by. Late in the month of Anthanos, the first snow of the year came falling down in large white flakes. And the next morning, we awoke to a half a foot outside. Meanwhile all the animals were stabled and warm inside the barns, and we had harvested plenty of hay for the winter.

Inside the house, we passed the idle hours by telling tales by the fire. Kitty and I had fallen in love. As the days went on, everyone excitedly looked forward to the Yule.

It was late in the month of Candlebright. Outside, a foot of sparkling white snow had fallen. And inside, Morris and I worked to keep the fire burning in the hearth all day long. Joan and Luther and baby Edwin arrived one day from their home in Bandon to spend Yule with family.

By night we all gathered in the living room, wrapped up in woolen blankets and warming our toes near the fire. As the snow fell outside in heavy flakes, and Kitty and I sat near each other on the soft couch, I knew I had never been happier before in my life. I had found my love.

On the first night of Yule, Morris and Bella joined in chorus began singing in a loud, joyous voice.

The whole family joined in, singing the carol chorus by chorus in their mismatched voices. Then Bella brought out some sweetbread from the kitchen, and warm milk. Yule was the most festive part of the year—we elves had no equivocal celebration, but

I enjoyed it just the same.

As we ate, we spent the entire evening playing games of dice and telling stories by the fire. Bella Coy served an endless supply of sweetbread and milk. Drowsiness slowly overtook us. By midnight, we were all stuffed beyond repair, and had fallen asleep—on the couch, on the floor and wherever we happened to be.

The next day Granny Coy stayed back with Edwin while everyone else went on an outdoors adventure in the wintry landscape. We donned the sweaters and scarves and gloves that Granny and Bella had knitted for us. We struggled through the knee-high snow until we came to a small, frozen pond in the middle of a wintry forest.

There we spent most of the day sliding about and slipping over the ice, throwing snowballs at each other, laughing and making merry. The day was icy, but the clothing kept us warm and comfortable. We played around, tromping through field and frozen fen until about dusk then headed back to eat a dinner of roast ham and milk. Night fell early in winter.

When I saw Mr. Coy going upstairs to take off his sweater, I saw I had found my opportunity. I had been waiting for this moment for a long time. Although I was very nervous, I knew it was now or never.

I said, "Hold on, everyone! I'll be right back," and rushed after him.

When I entered his room, I saw he was struggling to pull the sweater over his head. I waited until he had successfully concluded his task.

Then I managed to say, "Farmer Coy, I've got a question."

"What is it?" he said as he finally tore the thing off. He breathed a loud sigh of relief and tossed the thick woolen shirt on the floor.

I cleared my throat and realized how nervous I was. My stomach felt very light. "Well, Mr. Coy, I wanted to ask you…" The next five words I only barely managed to say. "May I marry your daughter?"

I could hear my own heart beating in the silence.

Mr. Coy turned around with a look surprise. For a second despair and humiliation filled me. Was that shock on his face? Was it disapproval? Perhaps I had made some horrid social blunder. Perhaps he would not only say no—perhaps he would no longer allow me stay at his house anymore. No, a human woman could not marry an elven man.

But then Morris's expression softened.

"Absolutely," the farmer bellowed heartily and smiled, his cheeks still rosy from playing out in the cold. "Like I said before, Nocturne. I like you. I like you a lot, and I'd be proud to have you as my son."

I couldn't help but smile back. "Thank you, sir. Thank you so much."

When Kitty had donned her nightclothes, and was about to go to bed, I entered her bedroom. "Kitteryn?" I said.

She turned around in surprise. She had a comb in her hand and her long auburn hair was dangling all over her face. "Yes?"

I knelt before her. "Kitteryn, will you marry me? Would you marry an elf?"

She looked surprised at first. Finally she said, "Nothing would make me happier in the world, Nocturne."

I climbed to my feet and put my hands on her shoulders.

There was one last thing to tell her; the one thing I had left out for the time we'd loved each other. "Kitty," I said quietly. "Have you ever heard of a creature called a vampire?"

She raised a brow. "There is a legend I've heard of," she said, "A legend of a lost tribe of elves, the druen… they live far away, and drink the blood of men by night. They are monsters. I've never believed it—it's just another ghost story. Why?"

"It is not a ghost story. And they are not monsters," I said. I paused for a brief moment, then added, "I am one of them."

She gasped. Her eyes widened. She took a step back and began to shake. She asked, "Are you going to kill me? And suck my blood?"

I tightened my grip on her shoulders and didn't let her step any further away from me. "I would *never* do such a thing, not in a thousand lifetimes!" I gripped her hand in mine. "I love you!"

"I know," Kitty said. "I do believe you."

"So let me rephrase my question, Kitty. Will you marry a druen?"

She hesitated for what seemed like minutes. A bit of doubt crept into my mind; she seemed taken aback in shock, in fear and in surprise, until I really wasn't sure what she was going to say.

"Oh, Nocturne," she finally spoke, "I would marry you if you were Death Himself."

I smile crossed my lips. We locked together in a fiery, passionate kiss. "Then we will be married soon," I said, and headed upstairs to my bedroom.

On the last night of Yule, over a dinner of roast ham and Stanbridge Wine, Kitty and I stood up, hands clasped together, and announced our engagement before the entire family.

"Kitteryn and I are to be married a week from now," I told

them, "At the shire chapel in Bandon Town."

Everyone began to clap and cheer.

"Congratulations, Kitty!" Joan said. Luther smiled and nodded in approval.

"Sounds like a good time and place to me!" thundered Morris, "Joan and Luther will definitely be able to come, since they live there. Now I'll get to work putting an extension on the west wing of the house, a nice bedroom for you and Nocturne, sweetie."

Kitty stood in silence for a moment. "That's the other thing," she finally said, "Nocturne and I wish to move to Galiope. He'd like to live in a larger town, you see… and he knows of an inn he can cook for. He will take good care of me. I'm sorry, daddy."

Morris's eyes began to moisten ever so slightly. They sparkled in the light of the candles. But he was strong. "It's all right, Kitty." His voice, despite his tears, was firm and steady. "You do what is best for your husband, just as Bella does for me."

"I plan on it, father."

The next Friday we gathered at the Church of Avelona in Bandon. Friends of the family had gathered from all across the shire to observe our wedding—of Kitteryn Coy's marriage to an elven man. Of her marriage to a druen, although none knew of that but her. Perhaps sometime I might tell Morris and Bella of my true origins as well, but today was not that day.

I dressed in the finest attire the shire could provide—a dark leather vest fitted tight around my waist, a loose green tunic made of fine-spun wool, a pair of brown trousers and some shoes crafted by Luther himself.

Kitty wore her mother Bella's old wedding dress, a white one that was nice enough for what her family could afford. It was not the dress of a princess. But when she walked into the chapel, and the trumpets pealed to announce the bride's arrival, I swore she looked just like Katrina, shrouded in white like a goddess.

The priest said a prayer not only to Avelona but to all the gods, that they might bless our marriage, so that it might endure forever. He asked us if we were both willing to marry, and we both said yes.

He pronounced us one; we kissed, and we had been bound by the cosmic powers of every god and goddess.

The church bells rang crisply throughout the town of Bandon. We had our feast at the Coy house, made love in my room, and began preparations the next morning to leave for Galiope.

A few days after our wedding Kitty packed her things into a carriage. I stepped in the driver's seat and I watched her as she bid her parents a tearful goodbye. She climbed inside I snapped the reins, and then we set off for Galiope.

We arrived in the afternoon, and moved into our new home: an upper story flat in Lonen Town. I would work for Omagon Naron at the Bloodmoon Inn, like he had offered weeks ago.

Kitty and I were happy. I knew she would grow old and die long before me, but for right now, I had found my home and my happiness, and that is all that matters.

EPILOGUE

Among the Galiopeans I am accepted. I have found my home. To this day I have never lived anywhere else. I never dream of moving away. I cannot leave.

People often say the druen are monsters and murderers. They dehumanize us; turn us into servants of demons in their wild and fabricated tales. Perhaps that is true, for the ghouls of Sardur. But I am not one of them. I am Dralynthi; Night-Song; proud son of Drassané and Drethori Rabaam. I am the druen who loved a human.

I am a son of Gilden. The blood of the Dark Prince runs through my veins and I cannot remove it, no matter how much I complain. And I have not given up my bloodlust, to this day. The Oath of Dandrinnas is too much for me to bear, and is only a fool's burden. Have I overcome the curse of my fathers? No; I have embraced it.

So what have I accomplished? By the dark gods, and by the good gods, I have found who I am.

My friends do not call me Dralynthi, anymore; nor do I speak Elvish, except when required, to those who refuse to assimilate; the human tongue, though less graceful and simpler, has become more beautiful than Elvish to my old ears. And no longer do I live in my homeland. I prefer the human tongue. So you may call me Nocturne, the son of the night.

I have sinned. I am not perfect. I have murdered, I have stolen, I have stormed a village without a moment's regret. But I like to think that my heart, though some say it does not beat, is far from dead.

—Nocturne Drethuli Rabaam, 1139 YE

ABOUT THE AUTHOR

Cursed at birth with a wild imagination, Andrew Cooper spent his youth dreaming of worlds more exciting than Earth.

He is a graduate of the Odyssey Writing Workshop. His stories have appeared in Morpheus Tales, Fear and Trembling, Residential Aliens and Mindflights, among others.

CONTACT THE AUTHOR

Visit **www.aj-cooper.com** to sign up for the newsletter and stay up-to-date on new releases.

Find him on Facebook at:

www.facebook.com/AJCooperauthor